LAWLESS PRINCES

A DARK, WHY CHOOSE ROMANCE

BLACK HOLLOW ISLE
BOOK ONE

DANI RENÉ

"He who fights with monsters might take care lest he thereby become a monster.

And if you gaze for long into an abyss, the abyss gazes also into you."

— FRIEDRICH NIETZSCHE, BEYOND GOOD AND EVIL

To the readers who prefer more than one alpha male... I bring you three!

And to my super amazing VIP supporters on Patreon - Daisie, Tai, Elisha, and Stacie! Thank you!

A super special thank you to Sheena for working on this story and helping me polish it to perfection!

PLAYLIST

Remember Me - Hinder
Another Way Out - Hinder
Holding Out for a Hero - Nothing but Thieves
Moonlight Sonata - Ludwig van Beethoven
You and Me - Yelawolf
Hate You - Jim Yosef, RIELL
Paint it Black - Hidden Citizens, Rånya
The Devil You Know - Blues Saraceno
In the Dark - Solence
Sinners and Saints - Andrea Wasse
Devil Inside - CRMNL
Hurt You - Living in Fiction

For the full playlist on Spotify, click here

Please note this is book one of two within this world. It ends in a cliffhanger, with a sneak peek into book two at the end! There are some scenes that could be triggering, so please proceed with caution.

PLEASE NOTE: This is a why choose romance, and it includes MM scenes as well.

PROLOGUE

JUDAH

Five Months Ago

My world came crashing down the day I watched my father take his final breath. It's a moment I never want to relive, but the vividness of the memory makes it far more difficult to forget. It replays at times without warning. I grew up in his shadow, but I also looked up to him. A hero with the hands of a devil. He taught me everything I know.

With every step I take towards the dungeon under the Venier mansion, I feel more alive because I know what's about to happen.

Black Hollow has become my salvation. With my best friends, I rid the world of anyone who isn't loyal, who doesn't keep the secret code we hold so dear.

Omertà.

Silence, as they say, is golden, and our hands silence those who can't keep their tongues from spilling secrets.

"Why am I here?" the arsehole questions when I step into one of the interrogation rooms.

My great-grandfather designed the dungeon. It comprises a long, underground corridor, stretching from the western edge of the house to the east, with interrogation rooms and holding cells spread out along both sides.

Implements adorn the walls of the fifteen interrogation rooms, which can cause the greatest torment to their occupants. Each of the cold concrete rooms has been designed for a specific type of torture. Depending on the crime, the punishment fits perfectly, and what's left of the tortured body is used as an example to those wanting to run their mouth off.

I secured our current guest against the wall in metal cuffs that hang from the ceiling. The bindings at his ankles keep him in place with his legs spread wide. As he glares at me, I can see his face is already bloody, but I don't feel there are enough wounds for what he's done. There should be far more. His one eye is slowly swelling shut, and I can't help but smile.

"I think you know why you're here, Angelo," I

tell him as Valen takes my left and Malachi stands to my right. "We need you to tell us about all those dirty little stories you've been spilling."

"I have said nothing to anyone," he spits back, anger and rage dancing a seductive symphony in his tone. Lie number one. "You may think you know me, but you don't."

"Oh," I say with a shrug, "I know plenty."

"I understand the need for secrecy," he tells me. "Please. The Lawless don't have to do this," he says...rather, he pleads.

I love to hear people beg for mercy. Mostly because I never show any. The thing is, once you offer one person any kindness, it leaves a poor example to any others who might consider breaking the rules in the future.

"Your little girlfriend has been taken care of by some friends of mine," I tell him. "But then again, she wasn't yours, was she?"

He knows what I mean. His family hired her to infiltrate my home. Females are much better at hiding their true intentions by using their powers of seduction. That's the reason women weren't allowed on the island in the past, but since those rules changed, things have become a lot more interesting. The little whore came into my home and stole secrets from me, and I have no doubt in my mind she told Angelo everything.

"She didn't mean—"

"When a woman walks into this house," I interrupt him. "She signs an agreement never to disclose anything that goes on here. The rules are clear."

"I know, I know," he mutters with a nod. "She didn't tell me anything." Lie number two.

It's so easy. Men like Angelo make my job far too fucking easy. It's as simple as stealing candy from a baby—there's no fight. It bores me. I much prefer when they spew venom back at me.

I pick up the pliers, and stepping towards him, I pinch his fat, lower lip between the metal teeth and press down until blood begins to spurt. His cries of pain are like music to my soul. Releasing the now torn skin, I step back and glance down at my shoes.

"You've made a mess, Angelo," I tell him, and there's no humour in my tone.

Lifting my gaze, I meet his cold, angry glare. There we go, the fighter is lurking inside him.

"I-I didn't do anything," he mumbles, his wound making it difficult for him to speak properly.

"I have witness accounts that tell me you've been talking to your girlfriend. You see, I'm not a stupid man, Angelo. I've been doing this for far too long to allow anyone to fuck up what I've built, and what I've earned."

"I wouldn't break the rules of the Lawless," he tells me. Lie number three.

When I stepped onto this island for the first time as a student, along with Kai and Valen, I didn't want to follow the rules that were in place for the students. And my two best friends didn't either. We became what the professors called *Lawless,* and the name stuck. When Emilio and Jordan joined us, we indoctrinated them into our group and easily fell under the same moniker.

With every word Angelo speaks, more blood spurts from his mouth, causing me to shake my head. When I raise the pliers to his lip once more, he winces. And the fighter is gone.

I suppose, once you accept you're about to die, there's no reason to fight anymore. Angelo knows there'll be no mercy shown for his disloyalty. It's not in my nature to be merciful.

I take a swing with the heavy, metal implement in my hand, slamming it down onto one of Angelo's knees, which earns me an ear-piercing scream. I don't like people who try to fuck me over.

Angelo sent his little whore in here to seduce me and my friends and suss out our secrets, and even though I didn't fuck her, Val and Kai did. She had a job to do, keep things clean and work alongside the rest of the staff on the property. She was instructed to obey the rules and was forbidden from entering our private rooms, which are usually kept locked, but she didn't listen.

I found her snooping in my office at three in the morning, gleaning details about our life she didn't need to know. The files she'd laid out on my desk included details of where our territories lie, where our contacts are, and information about The Agency —an elite task force who we call on when we need certain jobs completed.

As Angelo shakes and spews curse words at me, I smile. I've had my fun. Time for my boys to enjoy themselves.

"I'm bored now. Val, sort this out." I hand my best friend of twenty years the pliers, and stepping back, I lean against the cold, concrete wall. Watching Valen in his element has become something of a hobby of mine.

There are so many secrets hidden within the Venier mansion, and as Angelo's screams bounce off the dungeon walls, I consider what life would be like if I didn't have Kai and Val here.

I don't like to think about it.

When I befriended Valen and Malachi at the age of five, I never imagined we'd still be together, almost twenty years later, closer than we've ever been and keeping each other's most secret desires hidden. They're the only ones I trust, other than my brother, Jordan, and my friend Emilio.

Once Angelo is dead, the threat to our livelihoods and businesses is gone, so I turn and make my way upstairs to the living room where I pour a double shot of tequila and swallow it back.

"I think we've made an example of him," Valen says from behind me. "And we've learnt our lesson. No more women," he adds, which makes me laugh.

He's one of the biggest playboys on this island, and for him to want to swear off women is like me promising to stop killing. Yeah, that's never going to happen.

"There's no need to go to extremes, Val," I tell him. "I agree we won't employ any more women, but next time we want to bring one back here to fuck, we need to make sure they're not allowed to wander round. Send them home after the fact." I look at him and smile. "And besides, I doubt you'd be able to handle not having regular pussy." I offer him a wink, which makes him chuckle.

"And what happens when you get married?" Val throws the threat at me as if he doesn't already know that I don't want a wife.

I'm more than happy with my life the way it is. Adding someone else to our rather unconventional, secret relationship would only complicate things. And I don't like complications.

"There won't be any women in my life…long

term, I mean," I inform both my friends as they watch me.

It's not been that long since my father's demise, and soon I'll have to attend the reading of his last will and testament, which undoubtedly means there'll be more rules for me to follow.

"You don't know what your father has planned for you," Kai adds his insight.

My friend may be right, but even if my father was still alive, I don't see him giving me a wife to take care of. He knew what I'm like.

"Don't be so sure you will not end up with the rest of your life perfectly planned out from the grave," Val taunts me, forcing me to pour another double and drink it back in one gulp.

"Oh, I know. You could be right," I say as I turn to them both.

My father may have loved me, but he also had his own set of strict rules and plans for me. He was the Boss, and for me to take his place, I'm going to need to obey whatever the fuck he set out in his last wishes.

No matter what.

A TWISTED CONTRACT

JUDAH

BLACK HOLLOW ISLE IS A SPECIAL PLACE.

A small island off the coast of Italy, which has been in my family, the Venier family, for several generations and now belongs to me. It's where I went to university, and it's where Jordan, my younger brother, is now studying for his degree. I live in our family home on the island that my father left to me when he died, and I wear the name Venier with pride.

The buildings on Black Hollow Isle are Gothic in architecture, boasting turrets and stained-glass windows. The charcoal brick, offset by the Mediterranean Sea, might seem strange and intimidating to the regular tourist who looks out from the beaches of Sicily, but we've done it for a reason—to remind those who know of us that we're always here, always watching.

Our folks were good to Jordan and me, always offering support and advice when it was needed, but since they've been gone, all I can think about is taking up the reins from where Dad left off.

His last will and testament was clear—never let go of your legacy. And I don't intend to. But as my private jet lands and we taxi down the runway, I have a sinking feeling in my gut. I'm almost certain there'll be another surprise from Dad now I'm nearing twenty-five.

The family business is import and export. Our allies and clients are Sicilian mafia, and when they call, we answer without question. But that's not why I've travelled to the Italian mainland. I got a call from my father's lawyer yesterday, requesting my presence at his office. Usually, I'd have him fly out to the island, but he said there was something I needed to collect.

He didn't tell me what it was, even though I asked. I wonder if it has anything to do with the university that sits on the isle. My great-grandfather founded Black Hollow Elite when he was my age. He brought in faculty members from all over the world to teach the students extra-curricular subjects that don't get taught in regular higher-education institutions.

It's a private university that takes up half the isle

and only accepts students from families who show loyalty to the Venier family and our allies. You don't necessarily have to be blood-related to anyone who is already a Made Man, but you must show you're willing to do anything, and I do mean anything, to join.

Students who are accepted learn a variety of skills including different fighting techniques, how to go undercover to garner information from rivals, and even how to establish and maintain business relations with criminal organisations. Most of those who attend are specially chosen from around the world and brought to the island to study. The rest of the students who are admitted, though, have had to beg and plead to join.

We don't accept everyone. All the applications are considered, but we do thorough background checks before we decide who can attend. It doesn't mean we never admit those who try to take us down—it happens more often than we'd like. However, we have learnt how to deal with shit like that, and every enemy we do find pays the price.

Living this life leads you to be colder than most, but it also ensures our safety. Black Hollow is my pride and joy, a gift from my father, but as much as I enjoy running the university, it takes its toll.

Most of the students come from old money. Blue

bloods. And that's where the Lawless Princes—me, Jordan, Val, Kai, and Emilio come in. We are the rulers of Black Hollow Isle, and our small group of friends will do anything to ensure we stay together and are safe. We'll draw blood from our own family members if they are disloyal, disobey, or betray what's ours.

As the sun sets on a long, drawn out day, I disembark and head for the limo waiting to take me to my destination. Meetings are my least favourite thing, but with my father gone, I have no choice. I'm the eldest, which makes me the one who has to lead.

"We're here, Mr Venier," the driver says after sliding down the partition that separates us. "I'll wait." He's been with the family for so long, I don't remember a time I haven't seen him around the house and grounds.

"Thank you."

Pushing open the car door, I exit the vehicle into the sticky summer air. It's humid and I wish I was sitting on the beach with a handful of pretty women around me, rather than standing outside the offices of Hamilton & Associates in a fucking suit.

When Trevor Hamilton moved from London to Reggio Calabria to work for my father, he gave up his life for the Venier clan. Even though he has other clients, we are his priority, and we always will be.

Inside the air-conditioned office, I find a receptionist who looks as old as time. She glances up and I realise it's Hamilton's wife. I've only met her a couple of times, and I was much younger then.

"Mr Venier," she says with a kind, warm smile, and for a moment, I miss not having my parents and grandparents, but I quash the emotion quickly and offer her a nod.

There's no need to show emotion to anyone. The only people who see me *feel* are Kai and Val, the two men I trust the most with my life.

Any time an Underboss is about to step up into the role of the Boss of the family, he's watched like a hawk. Weaknesses can be exploited, which means I can't show any. I must be the cold-hearted son of the former most dangerous man in Italy. My father may no longer be around, but he's still remembered and feared. I want to be like that one day, and with each calculated move I make, I'm ensuring my name will be right up there with my father's.

"It's nice to see you, Mrs Hamilton," I tell her. "I have a meeting with Mr H."

I stop at her desk, waiting as she picks up the phone and taps out a number before pressing the device to her ear.

The woman is friendly enough, but I can tell she's not entirely comfortable with me standing over her.

It's something I've noticed when I'm around people —they look at me with fear, but there's also a hint of respect. I don't know if it's because of the name I carry, or if they've heard about the things I've done.

"Mr Venier has arrived, shall I send him up?" She listens for a long while before nodding and placing the receiver on the desk. "You're welcome to go up. He's in his office."

"Thank you," I offer before I leave her and make my way to the lift.

It's not a skyscraper, so the ride up doesn't take long. When the doors slide open, I'm deposited outside a set of double, mahogany doors. The heavy wood muffles the sounds from inside the office, but the moment I push them open, I'm met with two men I've never seen before as well as Hamilton himself. They're all seated, and their eyes land on me when I enter.

"Ah, Judah," Hamilton greets me by my first name, instead of adhering to the usual formalities.

He pushes to his feet and rounds his desk with a wide grin on his face. When he reaches me, he takes my hand in his and pulls me into the kind of one-armed hug I usually reserve for my friends. But I allow it.

"It's nice to see you again, Mr H," I say, keeping up the pretence of familiarity he so clearly wants to display.

I'm not sure who these men are, but something about them doesn't sit well with me. Whenever I walk into a room, I've learnt from my father to always take in every detail of anyone I meet. Whether they've got weapons, where their hands are placed at their sides, and if there's a hint of nervousness in their demeanour. The men watch the interaction between my father's solicitor and me with interest.

Hamilton leads me to a chair that's situated opposite his desk. From this vantage point, I can study the men in more detail. One of them is dressed in a dark, pinstripe suit, bright red tie, and a crisp white shirt. His hair is dark, and his eyes are as black as night. He pushes to his feet, holding out his hand to me. I don't move, because I don't know who he is and I don't trust anyone. I leave his hand hanging in the air, and when he realises I'm not going to shake it, he clears his throat as he pulls it back and nervously straightens his cuffs.

"Nice to finally meet you. I'm Mr Juliano," he says, his Italian accent thick around the words. "I work for Mr Saviatti," he informs me, and I quickly recognise the name.

Emilio, one of the Lawless Princes, is a Saviatti. He doesn't use the last name, and I don't blame him. If my father ignored the fact I'm alive, I wouldn't want any link to him either.

Allowing my knees to bend, I sink into the chair Hamilton offered me. My hands grip the armrests as I glance over at the man sat beside Juliano.

"And you are?" I enquire.

"Mr Saviatti. I'm Emilio's biological father," he tells me, shame dripping from his lips as he confesses something that makes my hackles rise.

I don't like this. Something is very off in this interaction, and I need to get out of here. But before I do, I'm going to get answers.

"So, you're the bastard who decided it's better to leave him with monsters than to care for him yourself?"

"Judah," Hamilton admonishes me, but I don't give a shit.

I'm not a kid anymore. I'm on a level playing field with this bastard, and I don't have to cower to him. I no longer believe in respecting anyone who doesn't earn it. You do good, I'll give you the respect you deserve, but if you're an arsehole, I'll treat you like one. And I won't feel an ounce of guilt about it either.

"No, he's right. I made a mistake when I was younger. Both my children deserve better than me, and that's why I'm here. To finally come clean and pay for my sins," the old man tells me.

His hair is greying at the temples, his face is gaunt, and the wrinkles under his eyes show his age. For a moment, I wonder if Emilio looks more like his mother, but then Saviatti lifts his golden eyes to mine, and I can see my friend's resemblance to this piece of trash.

Leaning back in the chair, I lock my stare on Saviatti, before asking, "What are you talking about?"

"Long ago, your father gave me an ultimatum," he admits, which has me scooting up straighter. He knew my dad. "I'd allowed my family name to become poisoned by the Camorra for many years before I fled. They'd blackmailed me into breaking the rules that'd been instilled in me since I was a young man. I needed an out, so I became an informant for the FBI."

"So, what? Are you here to beg for forgiveness? I'm not a Boss yet. I think it's best you talk to the other families directly."

"No. I mean... Yes, that's what I am going to do, but I need to settle the debt your father demanded all those years ago. He helped me escape the Camorra, and now I must repay what I owe. There was a contract put in place. He agreed to keep my son safe, which is why I didn't return to collect Emilio. It was the only way I knew how to keep everyone protected." The tone of his voice turns hard, angry, but then he sighs when I don't respond. "Your father was a good friend until I asked for his help."

"Help doesn't come free," I remind Saviatti as I sit

forward in my seat, and leaning my arms on my thighs, I tangle my fingers through each other. The pose is non-threatening, but when I lift my head, I notice how he takes me in with fear dancing in the golden orbs he pins on me. "So, what's the payment? You could've just transferred it to my bank account. I didn't need to be here for it. Oh, and I don't take cheques."

Hamilton steps from around his desk, his posture rigid as he brings a folder to my attention.

"This is the contract your father had drawn up, seventeen years ago." He hands me the document, and I quickly scan it. The letterhead is definitely the Venier coat of arms—a raven settled on a branch with a sleek blade behind it, encircled by thorny branches.

My eyes take in the wording and dates, then I flick to the second page that confirms I'm about to receive the payment whether or not my father is alive. It also confirms not *what* the payment is, but *who*.

My gaze snaps to Saviatti.

"You've got to be joking," I grit the words through my clenched teeth as frustration ticks in my jaw.

My father always enjoyed toying with me, testing me when he thought I needed it. But from the sadness on the old man's face, I can tell this is no fucking joke.

"It was an agreement I had to sign. It's what your father wanted," he informs me, his tone fit for a criminal, dark and foreboding, and my chest tightens.

Hamilton steps forward once more, and this time he hands me an envelope. "This goes with the contract."

He looks at me with pity in his eyes, and I want nothing more than to slice him, limb from limb, in my anger. He knew about this when I came here to listen to my father's will being read. Jordan and I stood, side by side, as we heard about our father's last wishes for us. And even then, Hamilton never offered me a look like the one he's giving me now.

"Why didn't you tell me before?" My voice is hoarse when I question him, and I have to clear my throat in order to find a firmer tone. "You knew, and you could've stopped this."

"There was no stopping what was set in motion years ago, Judah," he says, his answer not offering me any form of solace. Usually, I seek that kind of reassurance in the darkness at home, but right now, I'm looking for comfort in the gaze of my father's lawyer. It's not there.

I look over to Saviatti again. "What is your first name?" I ask.

"Emilio." He whispers my best friend's name as if it was a joke. A dark chuckle rumbles in my chest at his answer. "I gave him the one thing of mine I hoped he could be proud of — a good, powerful name."

I want to break this man in front of me. More so than I've ever wanted to hurt anyone else before. But as I fight to control my anger, the door to Hamilton's office opens with a soft hiss and the room fills with the scent of oranges, refreshing and sweet. Far too fucking delectable for me.

I push to my feet, my hands grasping the contract and an envelope that I'm sure contains a letter from Dad, telling me just what he has planned for me. Even from the grave, he's being a controlling bastard.

When I finally turn towards the door, I find my future standing on the threshold, flanked by two guards who look like they could break her in half. She's not short, but beside those two fuckers, she looks like a toy.

"This is my daughter," Emilio whispers, dragging my gaze from the brunette who's staring daggers at me. I glare at her father, his short frame standing beside me now. He looks like a broken man when he says, "She's now your property."

I don't know what to say, so I keep silent for a moment longer, and turning back to her, I take in her long, flowing chestnut waves and olive skin. Those same luminous, gold eyes of her father's watch me from a petite, pretty face. I fight the urge to go to her. To inhale her scent.

And then her father murmurs, "Please meet Brielle Saviatti."

THE WELCOME

BRIELLE

I'D HEARD ABOUT BLACK HOLLOW ISLE through whispers of my friends while living in England. Even though I left Italy when I was a young girl, I knew the island was notorious for taking young minds and turning them into monsters.

There have always been rumours, and even though I never wanted to listen to them, I realise now it prepared me for what I'm about to experience. All my life I've been taught not to show fear, and I'm trying not to, but I can't deny my nerves are frayed.

Over the years, I often wondered whether Papa would send me to Black Hollow, but what my future holds is nothing like I'd imagined. I'm not only going to university to get my degree, but I'm being sold off like livestock to one of the most infamous families. There has never been love lost between our two families, but with what my father did, it makes it even more dangerous for me to be around these people. They all know he's a traitor. The Saviatti name is infamous amongst the organisations, and it will be for years to come. The only chance for me to escape would be to marry outside the families, change my name, and move on.

But I can't.

I'm being thrown back into the deep end, and I'm going to have to learn to swim with the sharks. These are blood-thirsty predators who will not think twice about killing me.

My father ran from the mafia years ago and broke the number one rule—omertà. His return to them now won't be easy, and I have a feeling I may never see him again.

The four men before me stare as if I'm a circus act. My father and his lawyer, Mr Juliano, both have their heads bowed slightly, but I can tell their eyes are still on me. There's also the Venier's lawyer, Mr Hamilton, who's intently watching the scene playing out. However, the one man I've avoided looking at since I walked in hovers like a dark cloud on a summer's day, stealing the light. The man who, when I finally allow myself to take him in, steals my breath away.

When Papa told me about what's going to happen today, that I'd be meeting my future husband, I cried, screamed, and begged him to reconsider his decision. But he informed me the arrangement had been set in motion a long time ago. Once Judah turns twenty-five, he'll take over the Venier organisation, and the terms of the contract are clear, he has to marry me to do so. The only plus in this whole fucked up plan is that I'll be able to study and get my degree.

I didn't expect my fiancé to look as handsome as he does. Most men in the mafia are old and scary and look as if they could snap you like a twig while sucking on their cigars. But *him*, the young man before me is nothing like that.

Tall, over six-foot easily, he has messy brown hair that's long on top and buzzed shorter nearer the shirt collar. A few strands hang over his forehead, covering up what I can tell are soft hazel eyes, but they hold a hardness that causes me to pause.

His lips are full, pink, and I imagine them to be soft if I ever touched them. Which I won't. His angular jaw seems to be carved from the smoothest marble, and his suit is impeccably tailored to fit his broad, yet lean and muscled, frame.

His shoes even look like they're custom-made for him. Polished and expensive—he is a picture of perfection. But I know who he is, or rather what he is —a violent criminal. I'm pushed further inside the office by one of my father's men, and I have no choice but to move nearer *him*.

"Please meet Brielle Saviatti," my father says, his voice low, but it's heard by the entire room.

I stop a few feet from the group of four men, not needing or wanting to be closer. No matter what happens, I'll find a way out of this. I may need to obey right now, to keep the peace, but there's no way I'm going to allow my life to be owned by someone, even if he's a picture of perfection.

My father taught me to always get to know my enemies, that way I can defeat them. And that's exactly what I intend to do.

"I'm Judah," *he* says.

His lips tilt into a sensual curve as he murmurs his name, and I'm offered a dark, sadistic smirk when he holds out his hand to take mine. I don't fight him. I allow him to touch me, only to have my breath caught in my throat at the heat that passes between us.

I don't want to greet him.

I want to ignore him forever.

If I act like an insolent child, though, I'm sure he'll punish me. An icy shiver snakes down my spine with a warning to behave. If I don't make him angry, perhaps he'll leave me alone. Maybe he's not even interested in me. He probably only sees me as a problem. There is no other way to see me. I'm just someone to ignore, surely. He's not chosen me but been forced into this, and I know there'll be no emotion between us. No feelings. No love.

That's what I tell myself.

He's not interested.

The man before me can never be attracted to me. Which is fine because, right now, I don't like him very much either. And I don't want to like someone who's been forced on me. It's not natural. It's not how things should work.

I tip my head back, lifting my chin in a show of fake confidence and smile.

"I've heard a lot about you." My voice doesn't waver when I speak, and inwardly, I do a dance of victory.

I don't dare mention that those things I heard were scary and kept me up at night, wondering if he would ever hurt me, just like I heard he hurts others.

But then Judah leans in, his hand still gripping mine.

"I can't wait to learn all about you, little princess. I know the things your father has done, and I'm going to enjoy seeing if you've turned out like the bastard who raised you." It's a whisper, so only I can hear. And it's filled with a foreboding that confirms, once I leave this office, I may never see my father again.

Judah steps back, keeping his face calm, collected, and aloof. He's nothing short of a stone-faced nightmare standing in the real world, holding onto my hand so tight I almost flinch.

Almost.

I fight back the desire to run, to hide, to cry. Deep down, I want to scream and refuse to do this. I hold my breath, not wanting a connection with him, no matter how small. If I was to inhale his scent, I fear it would be the last thing I do before falling into his trap. He's a man with the means to hurt me...and enjoy doing it.

He turns to my father. "Any respect I may have had for you is gone. Your son, your daughter, all of those secrets you've kept from her are gone," he murmurs, glancing my way before flicking those hazel eyes back towards Papa. "She'll learn about the man she's grown up believing to be a hero. You've kept too many secrets, and now she's mine, I'll make sure she learns them all."

"What are you talking about?" I ask, still unsure of what he means when he says son. Papa doesn't have a son. I don't have a brother. "What son?" I question again, but neither of the men looks at me, which only irritates me. Deep down, I want them to acknowledge me. I'm not just a child forced to stay silent in a corner.

Judah ignores me while he picks up a folder from the desk and pulls a sleek, silver pen from the breast pocket of his suit jacket. He opens the file, and turning to the last page inside, he signs his name in an elegant scrawl on the thick, black line before handing the stack of pages to Mr Hamilton. My life has just been signed away to a man I hate. To a man who hates me. And there is nothing I can do about it.

"This is done." Judah's words are final. There's to be no debate about what's going to happen. "Come." The word is a command he throws my way before he walks towards the door. I don't expect him to wait for me, but when I don't follow, he stills. "Brielle, I'm not a patient man."

I look to my father who doesn't meet my gaze. "Papa?" My voice is barely a whisper, but he doesn't lift his face to look at me. Guilt creases his expression, but he only offers me a nod. "So, this is goodbye?" I infuse anger into my tone, which finally forces him to glance up.

"Tesoro," he pleads, and this time, he comes to me, and his hands grip my shoulders. "Forgive me," he begs.

Deep down, my gut churns, knowing this will be the last time I see my father. Because the moment he reaches out to the families, he'll be a dead man.

He won't be able to go back to the mafia.

They won't forgive him.

There are rules within the organisations—omertà means more to those men than anything else. Loyalty is something they value, and if you're unable to offer them that, you don't live.

"Goodbye, Papa," I whisper past the lump in my throat.

My eyes burn with unshed tears, but I don't allow them to fall before I turn away from him. He's taught me a lot in my short life, but the one thing that's always stood out is to be strong.

Faced with adversity and heartache, showing your weakness can be the fine line between life and death. I make my way to where Judah is standing and stop when I'm inches from him.

Tipping my head back to meet his questioning gaze. I take in the arched brow and the tilt of his lips that I'm guessing are perpetually shaped as if he's both annoyed and amused at the world.

"Hamilton, I will contact you soon as I have paperwork for you to complete," Judah addresses the old man. "I'll be in touch." That's all he says before he saunters out as if he owns everything he touches.

He's clearly used to getting what he wants. Confidence oozes from him, but also, there's a hint of danger that reminds me he's not a random, cute guy from school, he's the soon-to-be Boss of the Venier family.

I follow behind, not turning to look at my father. Instead, I step out onto the pavement where there's a black limo waiting.

The driver opens the door, and ushers me inside before Judah slips in beside me. The drive is quiet, with Judah on his phone for most of it. While he taps away on the screen, I steal moments to look at him, to really take him in. I know he's almost twenty-five, his birthday being three months from now, which is why the contract had come into effect.

He's focused on whatever is on the screen, so I shift my eyes over his long legs that are splayed out in front of him as he stretches the length of the back of the car. His black trousers seem to hug his powerful thighs in a way that makes my stomach somersault.

I don't *want* to be attracted to him, but if I must marry him, then I should at least feel something for him. *Shouldn't I?*

"If you keep staring at me like a little whore needing cock, I'm going to think you actually want to marry me," he murmurs across the space, his words tangling in my mind as they slowly twist around my heart and tighten until I can't breathe.

Anger rushes through me at his words. "Fuck you," I bite out, my hands fisting at my sides, which catches his attention. Fire blazes in those seemingly haunting eyes as he watches my reaction. "I'm no whore. Your father was a conniving bastard who thought he could rule our lives with a piece of scrap paper."

I shouldn't anger the monster, but my words hit home. He moves swiftly, and seconds later, he's right beside me, his fingers holding my jaw in a painful, vice-like grip. Judah leans in close, his warm breath fanning over me, causing desire and hatred to swirl together in a strange whirlpool inside me.

"If you ever speak of my father like that again," he hisses, his voice a low, menacing drawl, "I'll bend you over, expose your pretty arse, and I'll whip you so hard, you won't be able to sit down for days."

"I won't apologise for speaking the truth," I grit out through clenched teeth, locking my defiant gaze on his as the corners of his mouth tilt into a wolfish, sadistic smile.

Fear skitters down my spine. My breathing is shallow, my lungs struggling to work as his cologne captures my attention. He smells of warm leather and tobacco, a deeply masculine scent. And soon, all I see, all I smell, and all I feel is Judah fucking Venier.

"Don't fuck with me, little whore," he whispers close to my cheek, his tongue darting out to lap at my skin. It should make me cringe, but it does the complete fucking opposite. It makes my blood run hot through my veins. "I'm not one of those schoolboys you're used to," he informs me in a violent grunt. "I'm a man. And I will, most certainly, make you cry."

For a long moment, he invades my space, but I

don't fight back. Instead, I sit quietly, a small smile quirking my lips as he regards me with a penetrating stare. His mouth is inches from mine, the minty warmth of his breath has my tongue darting out to wet my lips. For a split second, his gaze drops to watch the movement.

My stomach twists with need.

Desire coils in my gut, low in my belly, until I'm squirming on my seat.

"Now," Judah says, "Be a good girl and sit quietly so I can finish my work. I don't enjoy being interrupted."

He pushes away from me, leaving me feeling cold and alone, and a shiver snakes its way through every inch of me.

Without him close by, I feel empty.

As if I've been cast aside.

It might sound stupid after what he said to me, what he called me, but my chest tightens as the car drives through the streets while he focuses on his phone.

I cast a glance out of the window, taking in the route as we head for the airstrip, and I wish with everything I have that my father would've just fought back. If he hadn't allowed guilt to eat away at him, I would be home right now.

But as we pull up to the private plane and come

to a stop, I'm convinced home is a place I'll never know again.

We exit the vehicle, the driver assisting me while Judah saunters in front. When we reach the steps, he halts his movements, then glances at me from over his shoulder. Those snake-like eyes lock on me.

His lips tilt before he says, "Welcome to the darkness."

THE TRUTH HURTS

BRIELLE

As the plane descends, taking me to my new *home*, I allow myself to wonder what life is going to be like. There's no doubt in my mind, going forward, there will be darkness, danger, and violence. Even though I've only ever heard rumours about the island, the university, and the students, it's as if I've been there before.

The moment the plane door opens, Judah is on his feet, looming over me with a look of thunder on his stupidly handsome face. He says nothing for a long while, merely taking me in.

"Time to meet the welcome committee," he informs me in a cold, detached tone.

This time, his mouth is curled in a sinister smirk. His full lips are distracting when he wets them, and I hate how attractive I find him. The pinkness of his tongue holds my attention as it slowly glides along the seam of his mouth, and I can't help the lust that heats my blood.

"I don't need a welcome committee," I retort, as I glare at him while I push to my feet. "I'm capable of finding my own way round."

My stubbornness is going to get me into trouble, I know it will, but I can't stop myself from goading him. My father always warned me about talking back, especially in our world. The mafia can't abide women speaking their mind. It's not how things are done. But my defence mechanism is to give back as good as I get.

Judah lifts one shoulder in a shrug. "What you want, sweetheart, and what you get are two totally different things," he mutters before leaving me on the aircraft and disappearing through the door.

When I reach the bottom of the metal staircase, Judah has already gone and I'm met by four guys all dressed in black. One of them is wearing a hoodie— the hood of which hides his hair from view and is pulled down just enough to cover one of his eyes. But the other eye is visible and locked on me. The stark blue that greets me is alarming—it's almost silver.

I take in the other three men, all looking at me as if they've never seen a woman before. But when I meet the gaze of the one on the far left of the group, my heart stalls for a few seconds. The gold of his eyes is softer than mine but still as intense as when I look in the mirror.

"Who are you?" The whispered question that falls from my lips is full of shock and awe.

Even as I ask, I already know. When we were in the office in Calabria, I recall Judah mentioning something about a brother, but I thought he was making things up to anger me. However, the young man in front of me is clearly related to my father, which inadvertently means he's related to me. My mouth opens, but I can't find the words to say anything to him, because even though he resembles my father, he's a stranger to me.

"So, this is the gift Judah's dad left for him?" the hooded figure says with a slight chuckle. He steps forward, pushing the material away from his eyes, and I'm swept up in the sea of blue. "Not bad at all." He tips his head to the side, assessing me as if I'm a possession to be sold, to be bartered. I suppose I am.

I turn my attention to the third man who's assessing me as if I'm cattle being sold at an auction. He's a similar height to Judah, but I can see his shoulders are broader and his body is bulkier. The jeans he's wearing hug his thighs. He hasn't spoken yet, but his look is intimidating, and the black T-shirt he's wearing reveals tattoos from his wrists to his shoulders and up his to neck.

My gaze shifts over to the last of the four. He

looks like a younger version of Judah, and the deep anger I've been holding onto since the meeting in the lawyer's office laces my question as I enquire again, "Who are you?"

"We're the Lawless Princes, sweetheart," the guy wearing the hoodie says before he slips the material off his head and grins. His smile brightens the blue of his eyes, and I take in his chestnut hair that's buzzed short. He looks like he should be a model or in a boy band—he's beautiful.

"I'm Jordan," the one who looks a lot like Judah tells me. "Judah's younger, but handsomer brother." He offers me a confident smirk, and I can see he looks even more like his brother with that expression on his face.

"You're full of shit," the guy with the hoodie laughs out loud. "I'm Valen, but you can call me Val." He holds out his hand, and I regard it for a while before accepting it. Heat sizzles through me when he brings my knuckles up to his lips and presses a kiss to them. "The pleasure is definitely all mine."

"That's enough," comes from the young man with golden eyes like mine, but I can't bring myself to look at him again.

Anger and confusion surge within me as I'm reminded that no matter how well I think I know my father, it's abundantly clear I don't. There are secrets he's been keeping from me, and it seems that the biggest one, my half-sibling, is standing a few feet away from me. I'm not sure what to say, because I feel as if the wind has been knocked from my lungs.

I want my father to explain himself, but I probably won't get the opportunity to see him again. When he said goodbye to me, there was a finality to it. The only thing I can pray is that he's still alive after he meets with the heads of the families.

Valen releases me, stepping back to allow my brother to step forward. I finally drag my gaze towards his, and I can't help but shiver. He looks so much like our father that it's strange looking into his eyes. There's no denying he's a Saviatti. He is my father's son.

"You're…" I don't know what I want to say. I'm not sure there are enough words to express what's roiling within me, so I stay silent.

"I'm Emilio," he says, and my stomach drops. This is Papa's son, but he's not my brother. I can't accept that he's my family. I had no clue he even existed until today. "It's nice to finally meet you, *sister.*" He emphasises my new title slowly, the word hanging between us, heavy and pained. "I wish things were different."

The one who's tattooed continues to look me over, but he doesn't say anything. It's Jordan who introduces him. "This is Malachi, but we call him Kai. He prefers watching to speaking."

Something tells me there's more to what Jordan just said than the innocent explanation in my mind. I take Kai in, noticing his tanned skin that's marked like a beautiful piece of artwork. His arms are pure, lean muscle when he moves.

Valen speaks from behind Emilio. "Let's go. Judah wants us in a meeting, and we need to make sure she knows where she's staying."

He turns and leaves me with my brother. Emilio tips his head to the side, gesturing for me to walk, and I have no choice but to follow him towards the waiting car.

Valen holds the rear passenger door open, waiting for me to slip into the seat. The interior is spotless, the smooth leather of the seats pristine, and when the guys all get in, I'm surrounded by their cologne. Each one different, but they all seem to mingle and fit together.

It's Emilio who takes the wheel, while Jordan sits beside him in the front passenger seat and Kai and Valen are on either side of me.

The drive is silent, tension hanging in the air, and I wonder if they're keeping quiet because they're each assessing me in their own unique way. Emilio turns left onto a road that seems to wind up a steep cliff.

"Where are we going?" I ask, glancing beside me to find Kai watching me.

His eyes penetrate through my defences, and a shiver of apprehension dances down my spine. I didn't even consider where I would live while on the island. I don't know these guys, even though one of them is my brother.

"Home," Val offers, and the two guys in the front seats chuckle.

But when I meet Kai's gaze, he gives nothing away. His expression remains neutral, a reminder that these men have been trained to be cold-blooded killers. I'm under no illusion—they'd willingly kill me without hesitation.

They are aware of my last name, and I know I'm not the woman they would've wanted in their world, which is what this island is. It's a piece of land, cut off from the rest of the world, where the violent and most dangerous men come to play. There are no rules here, only the ones that they make up for themselves, and something tells me these Princes don't play by those either.

Even though they own Black Hollow, this is still a place of learning, I reassure myself. However, I know I'm going to be one of the very few girls here. It's only in the past ten years that females have been allowed to attend the university.

"I thought I was staying in a dorm," I say,

confusion settling in my gut. I can't stay with them. There's no way I'll be safe in a house filled with monsters.

"Who told you that?" Emilio asks, glancing at me from over his shoulder.

I'm still struck speechless when I look into his eyes. The boy who my father left behind, only to take me to England and raise me in secret. There are so many questions I have for him. Did he know about me, and why didn't he come looking for me if he did? Maybe he didn't want to be sullied with the bad name I grew up with. Which in some ways, I understand. But it still hurts that I have a brother I didn't grow up with.

The silence is a palpable force in the luxurious interior of the vehicle. Suddenly, we come to an abrupt stop, and it seems we've reached our destination.

"Welcome home," Jordan says before exiting the car.

The other guys get out, and Val opens my door and offers me his hand, which for a long moment I consider refusing, but I sigh and take it.

"The Venier Manor in all its grand opulence," he announces.

I take in the mansion that sits atop a hill, overlooking a turbulent ocean. And I'm almost certain what goes on inside is just as volatile. The gravel crunches under my shoes as we head towards the monstrosity that is the Venier family home. It looks more like a Gothic castle where vampires live, rather than a home for the guys accompanying me. There aren't any lights on, even though it's getting dark outside. With winter coming soon, the sunlight is stolen by night early in the day.

When Papa first told me I'd be studying at Black Hollow Elite, he made it seem like a privilege, but nothing about what they do here is honourable. I did my own fair share of research and realised it wasn't a place I wanted to be. A university where monsters come to learn how to kill.

I also learnt about the young men who would soon take over their families, stepping up as Bosses. The Lawless Princes who rule over the island are drenched in secrets. Danger follows them like a shadow does a person.

Black Hollow Isle was acquired by the Venier ancestors as a place where they could bring unsuspecting victims and torture them. Soon after, a university was founded in one of the castles on the isle, and to this day it is renowned for its exclusivity, only accepting a select few young men, and now women, who show promise and loyalty to the clan.

Which brings me here.

Even though my father walked away from this life, his connections ran deep.

And for him to keep me safe, he had to sell me.

Val doesn't release my hand as he pulls me behind him. The slamming of the boot has me glancing over my shoulder to find Jordan and Kai carrying my luggage.

We make our way up to the intricately carved front door. The thick wood plays out a scene of five beasts surrounded by a throng of trees. These aren't wolves or bears, but men in hoods who seem to hide amongst the thick trunks. A brass skull adorns the middle of the door, sending ice through my veins.

Val pushes open the door and leads me inside. The impressive, black and white entrance hall encompasses two levels with a central, sweeping staircase leading to a long balcony on the first floor. The steps are tiled, and the bannisters have a smooth iron finish.

Contemporary art hangs on the walls, welcoming us into the immaculate house. At the top of the staircase is a large window that reaches up to the ceiling. A chandelier of a thousand crystals hangs above our heads, shimmering with a golden hue, illuminating the modern interior.

"This is…"

"Home," Val whispers in my ear sending heat skittering down my spine.

His hand is still in mine, and he tugs me up the staircase, taking the steps one at a time while I attempt to keep up. Once we reach the first floor, he releases me and heads towards a corridor on the left-hand side. I'm still behind him, and as he reaches the third door along, he suddenly stops, causing me to slam into his taut, muscled back. Even under the thick material of his hoodie, I can feel the tension in his body.

"This is yours," he says but doesn't look at me.

He pushes the door open and steps aside. The bedroom is nothing like I expected. Everything, well, almost everything, is off-white. There are hints of pinks and blues, but it's extremely girly. "This is the only room in the house that's yours and yours alone."

Spinning on my heel, I turn around, only to meet Kai's icy stare. "And everywhere else in this house I'm fair game?" My question sounds detached, and all four guys chuckle.

But it's Val who responds, "We all live here. Judah lives on the next floor up, directly above your room."

Flutters tickle my stomach at the thought. He's so close, the man I've been promised to.

"And you?" I whisper, keeping my focus on Val, but I can feel Kai's stare on me, burning into the side of my face as he watches my reaction.

Even though I try to keep calm, the tremor in my hands is enough of a giveaway to confirm his effect on me.

"Kai and I are also on the third floor," Val says, a smirk curling his lips. "If you need anything," he waggles his eyebrows, "just give us a shout."

"I think that's enough now, Val." Kai speaks for the first time, his eyes flicking between me and Val. The tension in the air between the three of us is charged with sexual energy. "Let's go," he says, and turning on his heel without so much as a look at me, he leaves.

I don't know why it stings, but it does. He's a stranger to me, but the fact that he's ignored me since we met at the airfield makes my chest tighten.

"See you later," Val utters, the promise in his voice has me shivering in anticipation of what's to come.

Once they've gone, I wonder if I'm going to survive this. Now there aren't eyes on me, the loneliness and anger take over. My father sent me here as a payment for a debt, and I have no choice but to survive.

The truth hurts, and I realise there's no other way to get through this, except to fight back.

If I don't, I doubt I'll come out of this on the other side.

A DARK VOW

JUDAH

WITH ENOUGH MONEY, YOU CAN OWN ANYTHING, anyone, you want.

It seems my father believed that till his dying breath. I haven't gone to see her, even though I was tempted to last night. Jordan came to me after showing her the bedroom and told me he thought she was intriguing. I can tell my brother is interested, but she was given to me. A gift my father thought I needed right before my twenty-fifth birthday.

I can't deny she's beautiful. There's something intoxicating about how she holds her own with me. I figured she would cower, but she didn't. Most women either fall at my feet or they run in fear. The whispered rumours amongst the students have always been part of my life. But then again, none of it is fiction, I am the cruel bastard they call me.

When the rest of the Princes arrived came home

53

with her yesterday, I wanted nothing more than to go to Brielle and introduce her to her new home. But I refrained, I didn't allow my curiosity to get the better of me.

Yes, she's beautiful, but she's come into my home as a stranger, one that I don't trust. I wasn't lying to her when I said I would make sure she knows who her father truly is, but that will come with time.

She's overwhelmed at present. I can tell from the glimpses I've caught of her. There's a nervous energy emanating from her. I've learnt to read people all my life, and I can see it in her. She needs to be clearheaded when I finally reveal to her the information I have about her father.

I can't allow my father's gift to distract me from running this place. I have to make him proud. Forcing me to bring her here is frustrating. My father died when I was twenty-one and Jordan was nineteen. He knew I'd chosen never to marry. My focus has always been on taking over the family business. Once I'm named Boss, I'll be able to leave the island. I'll make sure Jordan takes over my responsibilities here, and I'll return to the Italian mainland.

I know the history between Dad and Brielle's father, and I wonder if this was done purely out of revenge. If I'm to run the family, I'm going to need a wife eventually, but it still doesn't explain why he chose *her* in particular.

Women have always been my downfall, my distraction, but that's in the past now. Dad used to tell me that one day they would bring about my demise. The moment I hit sixteen, some pretty girl or another always swayed my focus. Father saw that— he noticed my attention could be easily stolen. But all that changed when he died, and I came here to run the university. I finally realised the truth. Yes, women are a distraction, but my best friends, the Princes, are my strength. The men I trust with my life. And then there's Kai and Val—we're much more than friends. We share everything between us, and now we have a woman in our lives. She will be owned by us all.

I hit send on the message to let them know I want to meet up this afternoon. I cancelled last night's meeting because I couldn't bring myself to talk about work. But I have pressing matters to consider—the first being the hiring of new professors. I haven't spoken about Brielle to Kai and Val since we brought her home, and I'm not sure I'm ready for it. She may be mine, but that doesn't mean shit, because she belongs to the three of us. And I can tell they're taken with her.

I settle behind my desk and pull up the signed contract from Hamilton. The terms are clear, I'm to marry Brielle before I can take over the family. I want to be Boss by my twenty-fifth birthday, which gives me three months. Ninety fucking days of learning about her before I say *I do.* It's archaic. There must be more to this stupid contract than meets the eye.

My office door opens, and Jordan saunters in. Dressed all in black, he settles opposite me, leaning into the chair as if he's exhausted.

"What?" I ask, turning my full attention to my brother.

Only two years younger than me, he has the mind of a killer and a body that's honed as a weapon. I can fight and hold my own, but my brother is second to none. I'm more business-minded than he is.

"Have you gone to see your little doll yet?" He smirks, resting his elbows on the arms of the chair, his fingers poised in a steeple as he rests his chin on the point.

Shaking my head, I glance at the contract once more before I say, "No. She can wallow in the comfort of her bedroom. I need to find out why Dad planned this shit."

Jordan settles back in his seat, watching me through narrowed eyes. "Maybe he wanted his eldest son to make some babies and live a normal life," he suggests easily, which grates on my nerves.

"I'll never have a normal life," I bite out, frustration ebbing and flowing through me, a river of annoyance that my brother could even utter those words. "I'll always be the head of the family. There's no stepping away, taking a holiday from it, and there is no denouncing my name. For the time being, the university is my focus, and some random little girl who thinks she's going to be a queen at my side will not make me love her. She will always be the traitor's daughter."

"You need to get some pussy, brother," Jordan laughs. "It's obvious you're wound so fucking tight. You cannot run shit while you're acting like this."

"Acting like what?" I push to my feet, leaning over the desk with my palms on the smooth wooden surface. "I'm trying to be responsible. To make sure we have a legacy to leave behind one day."

This time, my brother rises to his full height. He meets my stare, dead on, and I know this is an argument we'll have again and again. We have always butted heads about how to live our lives. He doesn't understand the responsibility, but even though we may argue, I love him and I would die for him. And he knows this.

"Who will care about the legacy when we're gone?" Jordan challenges. "After us, there's no one else," he tells me. "I love you, but sometimes you can be such an arsehole. Don't allow the privilege of running Black Hollow to turn you into Dad." He throws the insult at me without a falter to his tone or a glint of guilt in his eye, and then he turns and walks out of the office.

Besides Kai and Valen, my brother is the only other man I completely trust with my life. Emilio and I are best friends, but my relationship with him is more complicated because he's a Saviatti. I can't trust that he won't turn into his father. I've learnt that blood is strong, and if someone comes from a certain gene pool, they'll eventually follow in the footsteps of their parents.

Jordan has. So have I.

And when it comes to Kai and Valen, they're the same. Their fathers both run enormous organisations, and my friends are the spitting images of their parents, both in looks and how they live their lives.

I have tried to change some aspects of how I live my life. My father focused solely on work, whereas I have allowed myself to care for both Kai and Val. And since the day we took that last leap into our unconventional relationship, I haven't looked back.

Slumping in my chair, I blow out a long, deep breath, and even though I don't want to admit it, I know Jordan's right. Our father was far more focused on the university, making sure the students graduated with honours, than loving his family as a father should.

When my mother died, I think perhaps dad was almost relieved. Their fighting only got worse over the years. When she married him, she didn't realise he would always love Black Hollow more than he loved her.

The mafia came first. That was his life.

And if I have to be honest, as much as I want my father to look down and be proud of me, I don't want to turn out like he did—focused and alone. Sighing, I push to my feet, leaving the contract open for when I return. I'm caught between wanting more from life, but also not wanting to open my mind to more.

However, it seems my father was determined to force me to think about a family. There's no doubt in my mind he expected me to have children, and since he knew my views on women and matrimony, he took the decision out of my hands and ensured I would obey his wishes and marry. It rattles me, somewhat, that he's still ruling my life from the grave.

I make my way down the hallway towards Brielle's room. Her room is in my wing of the house, overlooking the university in the distance. Even though Black hollow is an island, it's a vast expanse of land that allows us to enjoy our games.

I grew up in Calabria, and when my father agreed to allow me to come to the island, I couldn't have been happier. I wanted to experience the reality of this life I grew up in, and I needed to know what my future entailed. When I first moved here at sixteen, I didn't attend classes like the rest of the students, I had personal tutors until the time came for me to go to Black Hollow University.

I matured, I focused, and I found I enjoyed the danger that comes from his life. There was no doubt in my mind, this is where I needed to be.

As wealthy students, we could afford fast cars, and that gave us the opportunity to amuse ourselves by speed racing through the streets and up the high cliffs, only stopping short of falling over the edge.

Every Sunday we would convene in the centre of town, and like clockwork, every student, new and old, would arrive in their sleek sports cars. But I, along with my friends, would always win. It's one of the reasons we became known as the Lawless Princes. We'd do anything to finish first.

The small town, sitting between the Venier manor and the university, provides accommodation for the faculty members and the security guards and enforcers who are here to ensure a mutiny doesn't take place on the island.

And that's where the fun came in for us. We loved the chase and being able to escape with a quick shift in gear. We still compete in the races, whenever we get the chance, but that's not as often as we'd like.

I stop for a moment by the windows that overlook the garden and I'm close to where I know Brielle is in her bedroom. I take in my domain, as a king would his kingdom. The title is one I have never truly wanted because I didn't need to be bowed down to, but over the years of being here, I've found my need to be King instead of a prince has grown. But I take the title of a Lawless Prince seriously. I don't obey the rules, I certainly don't listen to the law, and I make sure those who follow me are free to do as they please.

By the time I get to Brielle's bedroom and push open the door, without knocking, I'm calm. But what I find inside the room knocks the breath from my lungs.

As I stand in the doorway, Brielle screams, shock painting her pretty face crimson, and her mouth pops into an O. Her eyes are wide as she glares daggers at me and demands, "What the fuck is wrong with you?"

It's not her words that have my blood heating, though, it's her near naked body. She's only wearing a pair of black lace panties, her one hand covering her ample tits, and her long legs are bare, showing off smooth, tanned skin.

"How long do you have, darling?" I ask her, dragging my gaze slowly from her feet to her eyes. With each inch I devour, I notice her visibly shiver.

"Get the fuck out!" Her screech is cute. And I step into the room and shutting the door behind me. "I said—"

"If you continue screaming at me, I'm going to bind you to the fucking window and ensure everyone on the property can see those perky tits," I inform her coolly, twisting my cufflink between my fingers while imagining it was her peaked nipple.

"Fuck you, I'm not your property yet," she spits her venom, causing a smile to tilt the corner of my mouth.

It's been a long time since any woman has been brave enough to say something like that to me. Actually, most of them would fall to their knees in my presence, but Brielle is different. Trust my father to find someone fiery and defiant.

"I'm thrilled you said *yet* because once there's a ring on your finger and you're bearing the Venier name, if you ever so much as utter a defiant word to me, I will take you across my knee," I inform her, as I cross my arms and lean against the door.

"You're a joke," she throws back. "I'm here to study. You're just a complication in my life." Her voice lowers, and her tone turns sad. "My father should never have promised something that wasn't his to give."

Almost as if the fight leaves her, she pulls on an oversized tee, affording me a split-second peek at her perfect tits before her upper body to the top of her thighs is covered. I'm shocked to find I miss seeing the smooth skin that will most definitely feature in my fantasies when I'm alone.

"This life isn't fair," I tell her, thinking about my own future. I didn't choose her, but she's here, and I have to make the best of this situation my father threw me into. "Especially when you are a member of the familia. Choice is taken away from you and you're no longer your own person."

Brielle lifts her eyes. Those pretty gold orbs remind me so much of Emilio's. I still can't believe my father arranged for me to marry her. But looking at her long, flowing, chestnut locks, those soft, plump lips, and her watchful gaze, I don't think it's such a terrible deal.

"But I never wanted to be part of this life," she insists. "My father took me away from it and raised me alone. He risked his life to save mine, yet I'm now being thrown back into the darkness without a safety net."

Something inside me twists painfully, my chest tightens, knowing she'll never have a normal life either. We're nothing but slaves to our fate. And destiny is a frightful bitch. Serendipity and all that bullshit is nothing more than a lie. It's not there to be good to us, it's there to force us into lives we can never escape from.

"You're part of us now. The Princes will never allow you to get hurt."

I make her a promise I've never made to anyone outside my circle of friends. But it's true. No matter how she came into our lives, I have a responsibility, and so do my brothers. We may be immoral, but we're not out to hurt innocents.

"But don't mistake our protection for kindness," I tell her. "I still hate you."

DANGEROUS STEPS

BRIELLE

I HAVE SEEN NONE OF THE PRINCES ALL DAY. I SPENT most of my time in my bedroom, not wanting to take the chance I might bump into one of them. Judah instilled fear in my heart last night when he told me he hates me. Not that I should care, but I can't stop my chest aching from the knowledge.

Even though I already knew he didn't see me as someone he'd choose to spend his life with, I'd hoped we could at least be friends. But, I realise now that will never be possible with Judah. This isn't a fairy tale, so I shouldn't expect a happy ever after.

Sadness holds me hostage as I consider what's going to happen over the next few weeks and months. My life is going to change, even more than it has already, and it's out of my control. It feels as if I'm caught in a rip tide, and I'm being pulled under.

As night steals the day, I move through the

enormous house and come across a long, dark hallway on the top floor I haven't explored yet. Thankfully, it's silent. There's no one about, and I wonder what they're doing. There are a few doors along either side, and I wonder if this is where Judah and his friends hang out. Their part of the manor.

Even though I wasn't forbidden to venture around the house, I've a feeling I shouldn't be here. Call it intuition, but with every step, I feel as if I'm walking into danger. I should turn back, but curiosity burns through me, and my feet move of their own accord.

When I reach the end of the hallway, I look back over my shoulder and note just how dark it is. There are small fake burners fixed to the walls. They mimic flames, but I can tell they're bulbs, shimmering with a soft orange hue. They offer little light, which makes the hallway rather spooky as I move in the shadows.

Everything about this corridor feels old world. Gothic. It makes me think about the old horror movies I used to binge watch with Papa when I was still in junior school. Only now I'm in my own real life, scary story, and I can't stop my stomach from churning with worry. This isn't the best idea, to be wandering around alone, but I was bored and needed to get out of my room.

The cool air that sends a shiver down my spine makes me turn to see if someone is following behind me, but I'm alone. I breathe deeply, hoping to calm my nerves. But it doesn't help much. I'm going to end up finding something I don't want to, I'm almost certain. There are always secrets kept hidden in places like this.

Between each doorway, there are paintings that intrigue me. Most of them are scene scapes, but there are a few with depictions of epic battles. I'm about to go back to my room when I hear a sound from behind one of the doors. My need to know more about the men I live with overtakes me and I reach for the door handle.

I twist it gently, praying I don't capture the attention of whoever is inside. The door nudges open, and the sounds become louder. It's obvious what's going on inside from the moans, and I really should turn back, but I can't stop my curious nature. I inhale a deep breath before I push the door open further, and I'm thankful it doesn't creak, because I don't want to be caught spying on whoever's inside.

The moment I'm able to peek around the door and into the room, my breath hitches in my throat. On the enormous bed are Malachi and Valen, with a woman. Their limbs are all entwined, naked, their bodies writhing in pleasure. But what has my attention is the fact that Kai and Valen are kissing each other. Their mouths fused as their tongues dual. The woman in question is being fucked ruthlessly by Valen while she has Kai's erection in her mouth.

The scene before me is erotic and beautiful, and I'm lost to the ache between my thighs when a hand is slammed over my mouth. Surprise causes me to scream, but the sound is muffled and the three naked bodies continue their pleasurable ride still unaware of my presence.

Warm breath fans over my ear. "Are you enjoying the show, little spy?" Judah's voice, a deep and dangerously seductive rumble, vibrates through me.

I want to run, to hide, but he's got a tight hold on me. His free hand trails over my shoulder, and gently, he brushes over one of my nipples that peaks, hardening from just the slightest touch.

With the precision of a surgeon, his hand moves lower until he reaches the apex of my thighs. Ever so fucking gently, he presses against my mound, causing pleasure to zip through me like an electric current. The need that courses through me makes my body shudder, both in shock and desire.

He doesn't allow his fingers to tease me, he only applies pressure with the heel of his hand, and my hips move of their own accord. A chuckle vibrates through his chest and into my back, causing embarrassment to warm my cheeks.

I can't believe he caught me snooping, and I can't believe Judah caught me, of all people. The bastard is looking at me with far too much satisfaction. He doesn't trust me, and now this has made it even worse. I've no doubt he'll tell the other two about what he found me doing. And they'll all know I've been sneaking around their home.

"Do you like to watch, princess?" he questions, his voice turning husky, as we both take in the scene before us.

I've watched porn before, I'm no prude, but seeing this in real life is something else. Judah doesn't let up on his taunting, the moans are getting louder, and the gruff orders from both men inside the room send me reeling as I imagine myself in her position with both men's attention on me.

I try to respond from behind Judah's hand that's still clasped over my mouth, but he doesn't let me speak. Instead, as my knees buckle, he drags me away from the scene and down the hall, holding me close to him. Once we're far enough away, he spins me round, and removing his hand from my mouth, he grips my throat and slams me against the wall.

"I don't like spies. I don't trust you, and I don't want you in my home. You're nothing more than a fucking disloyal Saviatti," he tells me as he takes my hand and presses it to his chest. I can feel his heart beating wildly against his ribs. Then, he slides my palm down until I can feel the hard ridge of the bulge in his trousers. "This," he says, "will never be yours. And they," he gestures with his head down the hall to the room we just walked away from, "will do as I say. Don't think for one second you'll be like her. You're owned by us, but you're nothing more than an asset my father acquired."

"Fuck you, Judah, I'm not a possession, and you mistake my curiosity for something more. I wouldn't want any of you, even if you were the last fucking men on this earth." My words are spat with venom, but I can tell they don't have their intended effect.

He chuckles at my outburst, and I can't ignore the fact my hand is still on his hardened cock—there's no denying the size of it would break me in two. Suddenly, he rips my hand away from his erection and shoves it above my head and against the wall behind me. His hold on my throat doesn't waver as those darkened orbs pierce me, holding me hostage.

"Let me make something very clear," he responds, his voice low and threatening, "There will come a time when you realise we're your saviours. Being on this island doesn't ensure your safety, especially when the other students discover you're living with the Princes. And another thing, pretty little spy, one day you will beg me for my cock. You'll be desperate for it, and when I don't give it to you, you'll get on your knees and beg for it like a little whore, just like all the other girls."

"I'm not one of them," I throw back easily. "And

let *me* make something very clear." Using his words, I lower my tone. "I don't beg for something that men offer me freely."

I don't know why this comment would make him angry, but his fingers tighten around my throat to the point where my eyes water. My free hand shoots to his, and I try to claw his fingers away, but it's no use. The focus of the gaze he pins me with is enough to tell me there's no way I'm getting out of his vise-like hold. He could snap my neck right now, and I won't be able to stop him.

He releases my other hand, and I snatch it away and attempt to pull his grip from my neck. I can't. He's too strong. Judah tips his head to the side, regarding me with interest as the corners of his mouth tip upwards into a cruel smirk.

Black spots dot my vision, and I know I'll pass out soon. Even though I can hold my breath for a minute, this is taking its toll. Leaning in, his lips feather along my cheek and his teeth graze over my earlobe, then he whispers, "This is a dangerous world, Brielle, and if you don't abide by the rules, you'll pay dearly for it."

My legs wobble as his words slowly sink in, and he finally releases me from his harsh hold. I sink to my knees and drag in a breath of much needed air. My lungs work quickly as my vision returns to normal. But Judah doesn't leave. He watches me on my knees.

I tip my head back. My glare snaps to his face, and his mouth turns to a full-blown wolfish smirk. I didn't take note earlier that he's wearing a pair of black trousers and a shirt that's half unbuttoned. The material offers me a glimpse of his smooth, tanned chest. Dips and peaks of muscle tease me, and I want nothing more than to stab him with something, to make him hurt, but he's right, the more I fight, the more they'll push back.

"You look good on your knees," he tells me nonchalantly as he steps back and takes me in fully. I shift to my feet, standing to my full height before he gets any other ideas. "The next time I find you wandering around where you shouldn't be, I will make sure you regret every moment of your spying."

"I wasn't spying," I tell him. "I wanted to explore my new home. Is that a crime?"

"Exploring your new home?" he mimics my words. "Is that what you call watching them fucking?" This time, he chuckles. "They don't mind an audience, but only with prior permission."

"It was an accident."

He takes a step towards me, causing me to flinch. But he doesn't come too close. "Is that why you're pretty little cunt is wet?"

"You're vulgar," I snap as I turn to walk away, but

his hand shoots out and grips my arm before I can escape.

"Don't ever think you're safe within these walls," Judah tells me. "We may protect you from the outside world, which is our duty, but we're just as dangerous as those out there. Our secrets are locked within this home, and you need to hold them as close as we've done all these years. Even though you've been given to *me* in a contract," he says slowly, "you belong to us all."

"I don't need you to save me. I'm not some damsel in distress. And you may think otherwise, but I'm not about to run my mouth off to anyone."

"Oh, and I am definitely no hero, little spy," Judah tells me, but I knew that already. He releases me then, and turning, I begin to walk away, but not before he calls out from behind me, "And don't forget, the next time you fuck up and make me angry, I like seeing you on your knees."

I don't offer a retort, because it won't have any effect him. He won't feel the hurt. Someone like Judah only responds to violence, and I know I can't fight him, not right now anyway. Perhaps I'll have to make the most of being here and train like the rest of the students.

I've heard of the archaic lessons at the university where the young men are trained to become soldiers who can kill at the drop of a hat. It's where they come to terms with the fact that their future's already laid out for them, and their choices are taken away. They no longer answer to God, they answer to the Boss or to a Capo.

By the time I make it back to my room, anger has blossomed in my gut. I will learn how to kill, and even if Judah won't allow it, I'll find a way.

The female students on the island aren't allowed to learn combat, but they can learn skills that teach them how to infiltrate organisations. In the real world, we are seen as normal citizens, on the island, we're the princesses of our clans. We're all from the same violent and destructive world.

I flop onto my bed and stare up at the ceiling. As much as I want to leave, I know I can't. I'm not at all a violent person. I couldn't even kill a spider if it came into my home, let alone a man who is almost double my size, but for now, I'll play their game. I'll be the dutiful student and learn how to kill a man without flinching.

I roll over, and Judah's words slam back into my mind, *You will beg me for my cock.* He has a high regard for himself. But then again, he's used to the rest of the female population on this island wanting a piece of the future Boss.

I don't want to admit to myself I was turned on by him. I'm not blind, though, he is good looking with his sharp angular jaw, smooth tanned skin, and green eyes that seem to shimmer with devious intent. And then there's his messy black hair that falls into his eyes, making him seem less threatening when he smiles.

Everything about him is a trap. He lures you in, and then, when you're lost to his beauty, he snaps and you're nothing more than prey in his clutches. And, I have no doubt, Judah Venier will devour every inch until there's nothing left.

I can't allow him to get to me. I can't allow any of them to get to me, including my half-brother. Everything about this is wrong. I can't believe my father would allow them to take me. It seems I'm nothing more than a pawn to them all.

My eyes flutter as exhaustion takes hold of me. If I manage to escape from here, I know I'll have nowhere to hide—the mafia will find me. But that doesn't mean I won't try.

I want my freedom. Even though I may have to take a few dangerous steps to get there. One day, I will walk away from this life, whether they like it or not.

DISCOVERING DESIRE

VALEN

THERE'S NOT MUCH I WOULDN'T DO WHEN IT COMES TO the organisation. The familia are more important to me than anyone else. I grew up in a world of vows and violence, where blood is used as ink when we sign our contracts and agreements. I've come to terms with the fact my future has been laid out in front of me. There are no choices in this life, because you do as you're told.

The moment I leave my bedroom and head down the hall, a whiff of sweetness hits my senses and I remember we have a pretty girl in our midst. The fact that she's Judah's means nothing. Judah, Kai and I share everything in this house, and she'll soon come to learn that.

It started innocently enough. We knew the judgement that would arise from our families, especially our fathers, so we've kept it quiet. They know of our exploits, there's no hiding that, but what they don't know is that our sharing is far more intimate than they would like.

I turn the corner and slam into a soft, pliable, feminine body that I reach out and grab before she can tumble to the floor. Glancing down, I take in our pretty new toy's face. A doll. She reminds me of those porcelain dolls that my mother used to collect. Perfectly created to taunt men like me. And I'll gladly play a game with her, enjoying the gentle caress of pink on her cheeks and the way her eyes dart back and forth with uncertainty.

"I-I-I'm sorry," she mumbles, dropping her gaze to the floor.

Her long, dark lashes flutter against the apples of her cheeks. There is a fragility to her, it makes her seem innocent when the gentle pink hue colours her face. So very breakable. There's no doubt this delicate beauty will shatter between us. And my dick throbs at the idea. It would be my pleasure to see her come apart at the seams, to see her break, only to put her back together again.

She doesn't realise I saw her last night, watching Kai and me. I thought she'd run off in shock, but instead, she stood at the bedroom door until Judah dragged her away. I heard him, felt him. There is an innate connection between us all, and I was more focused on her and him than on the woman who was trying to pleasure me and my best friend.

Kai will always do it for me. Cristina was just a vessel I could use at the time.

"Where are you going?" I ask, releasing Brielle from my hold.

She's dressed in a pair of skin-tight jeans and a cropped top that offers a peek of her tanned stomach.

"I have orientation in an hour," she tells me, and I want to go with her, to keep her safe from everyone who could bring her harm. I need to protect her because she's not only Judah's possession. She belongs to all three of us.

However, my schedule is already filled with classes. I'm not a student at the university anymore. I provide the combat training. I show these young boys how to kill. And I fucking love it. As much as I hate the rules we must follow, I was born to do this. To take a life, and to train others to do the same.

I want to ask her if she enjoyed the show last night, but I don't.

Instead, I say, "I'll drive you in."

I offer, wanting to keep her safe. She's beautiful, exquisite actually, and there's no denying I can't wait to have a taste.

She tips her head in frustration, which causes me to smile.

Then she throws back, "I don't need—"

"There's no debating this, Brielle. When one of us tells you something is happening, it will happen," I inform her. The contract is clear—she's to marry Judah, but that means nothing. It's merely a business agreement. She belongs to all of us. She's a possession. Ours to watch over. "And we won't allow you to leave this house alone."

"I'll drive her in," Emilio says from behind me.

Glancing at her half-brother from over my shoulder, I nod.

"That's fine. Make sure she's home right after classes."

I don't need to explain to him why. He knows the dangers that lie on the island, and he knows that if something was to happen to her, Judah would lose his mind. There are no feelings involved, but the one thing I know about my best friend is that he doesn't take kindly to having anything he owns hurt, broken, or stolen.

"I'm not a—"

"Brielle," Emilio sighs her name. I can read the frustration in his expression as he regards her. "Just listen to us," he says. "I'm not trying to play happy families with you, but you have to realise this island is full of up and coming soldiers, Capos, and Underbosses. They won't think twice about making you pay once they learn your name."

It's true. Her father is responsible for most of their

fathers going to prison. When he defected, he sung like a fucking canary. Everyone knows who he is. We can't hide who she is from the rest of the students or the faculty, but if they know she's property of the Princes, they'll think twice about trying to hurt her.

We're in charge, we set the rules, and we break them whenever we choose.

"Then why are you still alive?" she throws back, her glare pinned on her brother.

I want to chuckle at her fire. There's something intoxicating about a woman who can hold her own, and I wonder briefly if she'd be up for training. I doubt Judah would want that, though. None of the female students at the university are allowed to fight or learn the combat techniques we do.

Personally, I think it's archaic, most times women can infiltrate organisations better than men. Beauty certainly comes before brawn.

"Because I'm one of the Princes. They can't touch me," he tells her. "If you want Valen to take you to the campus, that's fine, but you're not to go out on your own."

"You're not my father," Brielle grits. "I don't need you to regulate every aspect of my life. I've lived long enough under Papa's supervision to know how to look after myself."

"Okay," I step in before all hell breaks loose and she ends up running away. Even though she can't get off the island, there are a few places she can hide. Not that I'd tell her that. "I'll take her."

I look over at Emilio who's currently at war with himself. I doubt he wants me anywhere near his sister, but he has to know she's Judah's girl now. And that means she's mine and Kai's as well. It's no secret we share everything.

"Fine," he appeases. "I'll see you in class," he informs her coolly before making his way out of the house.

Moments later, the engine on his Maserati roars to life and the tyres squeal as he pulls away and down the drive. The need to sigh is immense, but I tamp it down because I have to be the level-headed one. We're all on edge having Brielle here, and it's not going to help if we're fighting or arguing about shit.

"I need to get my bag," Brielle tells me before leaving me in the entrance hall.

I can't stop myself from watching that sweet arse as it sways up the stairs. Not long after she disappears, Judah appears, a smirk curling his lips.

"Desire is a dangerous emotion," he says as he reaches me. "You may think it's safe to indulge, but it comes at a price. And you may not want to pay it, Val."

I know he's attracted to her because he'd be blind not to be. Brielle is a gorgeous girl, so there's no reason for him *not* to want her. But Judah is stubborn as well, which means he's going to fight it as much as he can.

I've known Judah my whole life, and I've watched him wage war with his desires. He only gave in when he realised there is no stopping what the heart wants. The three of us—me, Kai, and Judah—are in this together. I step up to him, our bodies flush, and the hardness of his chest presses against my own.

The air turns electric when I lean in, my mouth at his ear, and I know he can feel the warmth of my breath. "Are you talking about me, or you?" I ask as I glance at him, my own smile curving my lips.

I've known my best friend for years, since we were born our families have been linked. Our mothers grew up together and were as close as sisters. When they married, it was a double wedding, and then we came along.

"I'm talking about all of us," he says. "She's dangerous."

The warning in his tone has my hackles rising. He must know something about her I don't because I thought she seemed more afraid of her predicament than dangerous.

I flick my gaze to his. "What do you mean?"

He meets my stare and says, "I don't want this girl to break our family apart."

"What makes you think she'll do that?" I ask,

confusion creasing my brow as I watch his expression.

If there's something I need to know about her, he needs to fucking tell me.

"I don't trust anyone. You know that," Judah says, and I nod. It's no secret. "I need to gauge her interest in us before I can make a decision."

"You can't want to kill her?" The surprise in my tone is evident.

The corners of his mouth tip upwards. "If she's a spy, then we need to eliminate her. That's the rule. The problem is, I've already found her in places she shouldn't be," he whispers. "I don't like it."

"Because she was watching me and Kai fuck?" Even as the question escapes my lips, I realise there's more to this, but it has nothing to do with her. "Are you jealous she was watching us?"

"No," his answer is swift, and it's a little too quick for my liking, but I believe him. There is something else bothering him about her, something he may not yet want to divulge. I know Judah, I can read him like a book, and his eyes confirm he's telling the truth, but I can also see that something is worrying him. "If she wants my dick, she'll have to work for it."

"Oh, brother, I doubt she will. There's a fire inside her. She's not going to beg for anything." This time, I can't help but chuckle at him.

"I'm not deaf," Brielle spits as she reappears. "Even if your dick was the last one on Earth and mankind was heading for extinction, I wouldn't want it," she throws at Judah, who's anger burns in his gaze.

I can tell the rage has overtaken him, but the schooled expression on his face gives nothing away. The man is a statue, made of ice and stone.

"Let me make something clear," he says, his tone confident as he speaks. "You are mine. You've been given to me as my future wife, and that means you'll take my cock whether you like it or not."

I shouldn't be hard as fuck right now, but I am.

Brielle's mouth pops open in shock, her eyes blazing with anger. "Fuck you, Judah. If you think your cock is coming anywhere near me, you're wrong."

Judah moves quickly, his hand wrapping around her slender neck as he pushes her against the pillar.

"If you speak to me like that again, I *will* make you cry," he sneers as he leans in. "And I like tears," he whispers against her ear. "I love to feel them drip on my cock, drenching the shaft so I can fuck you with it. I'll make sure you're claimed before you have time to spread those pretty legs for any of the other men on this island. You were given to me, and if you don't like it, then I suppose you could *try* to run."

The emphasis on try is clear causing Brielle's eyes

to widen as she glares at him. Even in her predicament, she's still fighting in her own way.

"But we will always find you," I say as I step up beside them and grip Brielle's arm. I need to defuse the situation. Judah releases her and moves away.

"Call into the office when you get back," he instructs me as he turns on his heel and leaves me alone with the trembling girl.

"He's a bastard," she tells me and I chuckle.

"That he is," I respond with a nod as I head out the door, her soft footsteps following behind me. The weather is clear today as I make my way to the drive where the vehicles are all parked beside each other.

I open the passenger door of my matte black Jeep, and helping her into the seat, I inhale the scent of her perfume that reminds me of warm summer days. I grew up in Italy where fragrances would assault me daily. There are different smells I associate with particular times of my life, and Brielle is bringing back memories of when I was still innocent. When I didn't have blood lust ruling my actions, and I didn't know what it was like to kill a man.

In the driver's seat, I flick on the stereo, and the vibration of the music thumps out of the speakers and through the leather of the seats. I don't miss how she squirms, and a smile curls my lips.

I want to reach over and run my fingers along her thigh, to see how much she's affected by my touch.

The dynamic between me and my friends isn't easy to accept, which is why we've kept it a secret from our families. Deep down, I wonder if Brielle will want to run when she finds out the truth, that she doesn't only have one man to contend with, she has three.

I know Judah has concerns, but we will get through it together. I have no doubt at all. The question is, will she accept it or not? And I wonder if Judah is more concerned about us falling for her and those emotions changing our relationship.

We don't speak as I drive her to the university on the other side of the island. It's not far, but the trip is long enough for my attention to be completely stolen by thoughts of her. I want nothing more than to delve into her mind and find out what makes her tick. It's going to take a while, but I'm determined to learn about the beauty beside me.

By the time I pull up to the front of the building, ensuring every student in the vicinity turns to look at her getting out of my car, I smile.

She'll have to get used to being the centre of attention. Now they've seen her with me, though, she'll be safe until she reaches the office to grab her schedule. Then it's up to Emilio and Jordan to watch over her until I pick her up this afternoon.

"Thanks for the ride," she says, a smile tilting the corner of her pretty little mouth.

"Anytime, baby doll," I say. "I'll collect you here at three," I inform her as I pull away, not giving her a moment to respond.

Even though I want to wait until we find out more about her, I can't stop the thoughts of having her beneath me, between all three of us, from plaguing my mind. Fighting desire is a losing battle. And I don't really want to win that war anyway.

By the time I get home, I'm tense, and I still have to talk to Judah. I know what he's going to say. And I'm not in the fucking mood to hear it.

HIDDEN THREAT

JUDAH

I DON'T LIKE HAVING HER HERE.

No. That's a lie.

But with the sweet scented temptress under my roof, I need to be vigilant. There are things about her I don't yet know, which has made me obsessed. It's not even been seventy-two hours, and I'm already thinking about her all day and night.

My plan is to search her belongings. I should have my soldiers go through everything, but I'd rather do it myself because I know I'll do a better job. Or perhaps, deep down, it's because I know she's ours and I don't want anyone, other than me, Val, and Kai, touching her things.

I can't trust her, which puts me on edge. She's in my home, in a place I consider my sanctuary. I can't stop wondering if she's hiding something. I've learnt that not all spies are made the same. Women often have the upper hand—they can use their beauty to draw attention away from what they're really doing. Dad warned us, Jordan and me, about how women are able to infiltrate organisations without anyone suspecting them.

Emilio may be Saviatti's son, but he's also one of my closest friends, and he grew up with me, she on the other hand was saved by her father. I still don't understand why Saviatti would agree to my father's contract, to bringing her to Black Hollow and back to the life he tried to free her from. And that's what I need to find out.

When Valen returns, I glance up to see him saunter into the office.

"Are we going to talk about the tension in the house?" he asks as he settles into a chair across from my desk.

I knew he would bring this up, but I'm not ready for that discussion. I don't think I want to admit, even to myself, this girl has got under my skin with her smart mouth.

"No," I tell him because I know he won't give this up until I respond. "But something isn't sitting right with me," I say as I open the email from my father's lawyer.

When Dad got sick, I didn't want to accept it. And even now, I'm still struggling with his death. I never let anyone know what I'm going through.

Showing emotion is a weakness, and I can't afford to let my enemies see me in that state. However, as much as I try to hide my pain, Valen and Kai see through my cold and poised exterior. They always do.

I look up from the computer screen to find Val's gaze locked on me. It burns a hole right through the darkest parts of my soul.

"What?" My voice is tight, and there's tension racing through me. My muscles are taut, and my gut is churning.

He shakes his head. "You think there's a threat to the university and island?"

His change of subject from Brielle is welcome. We need to focus, not on the pretty little spy, but on what lies ahead. Because in three months' time, I'll have to step up into the role of Boss. My father's last will and testament made it clear that when I turn twenty-five, everything will be given to me.

The university, the island, and the organisation.

The prince becomes a king.

But with that title, there are always prices to pay. Ones that will determine if I become ruthless like my father, or I turn over a new leaf. Something deep down tells me I've been taught by him for too long not to be like him. And if I'm honest with myself, I admit I quite enjoy it. The darkness that swallows me whole when I'm on a job or interrogating someone, and my thirst for blood—it all culminates in turning me into the old man.

"Gut feeling," I tell Val, who's slated to take over from his father in a few months, so he understands the pressure that lies heavily on my shoulders right now. "The agreement in my father's will to bring Brielle here makes no sense. Her father took her away from this life after defecting. Why would he then send her back? And why would Dad want her here?"

Val tips his head to the side as he says, "We can't ask her, because if she's a spy brought in under the guise of an arranged marriage, she won't say anything incriminating." He regards me for a moment then says, "The only thing we can do, is to investigate her past. We know they lived in London. Perhaps she and her father had connections there to some of the families who remained loyal to him. If Brielle knows anything about her father's dealings, it will be through those connections."

It's an idea. I can have men follow Saviatti, and I can have someone look into any communications he's been making.

"I'll call The Agency," I tell Valen. "They can have a team out within the hour. The more we can find out the better. In the meantime, I think we should keep her close. Her father is undoubtedly going to be meeting with the Bosses, and when he does, I want to know what's said."

"Saviatti did give her to you as if she was nothing more than a bartering chip. Perhaps this has something to do with your father. There could be so many reasons we can't see, yet." Valen shrugs as he looks at me, the worry in his eyes clear.

My best friend is right—he tends to be right more often than not. He's also level-headed and doesn't fire back quickly. Instead, he'll ponder something and look at all possible angles before acting. For someone who loves the kill as much as he does, I'm surprised just how composed he can be. Perhaps he works out all his frustration on the bastards we torture.

I enjoy inflicting pain, weeding out information by any means necessary, and the men on this island know that. They won't ever overstep where I'm concerned. I've earned the respect and fear of those around me. And I'm proud of it. But Valen has a blood lust unmatched by anyone else in our circle. It's what makes him special.

"Her father's still alive," I tell Valen. "What makes you think he hasn't planned this? He could have sent her here to gain intel. The bastard became an informant, went into WitSec, and now he's allowed his daughter back into the lion's den."

My office door swings open, and Kai saunters in as if he owns the fucking place. We're all three the same age, Kai turns twenty-five a few weeks after me. The only difference is, he'll remain Underboss for a while longer because his father has a hold on their organisation and doesn't want to let go.

"What's happening?" Kai asks, settling down on the red-wine coloured sofa that creaks as the leather bows under his weight.

The bastard is six-two, just like me, but he's broader and heavier set than I am. It's all the time he spends in the gym. I'm a runner, whereas Kai loves the heaviest of fucking weights. He's managed to bulk out, building muscle, and I can't deny, he looks good.

Val prefers fighting. Any martial arts he can learn, he will, and he does it fucking well. It's given him a slim physique with taut, toned muscles. We're all three very different, but also, we have so many similarities.

"Judah was just telling me about his concerns over the pretty little thing we have in our home," Val says with a sly smile curling his lips. Bastard.

"Oh?" This has Kai perking up. "So, this is about the fresh pussy we have to play with?" He laughs, and his eyes narrow, crinkling at the sides.

My frustration with both my friends is at an all-time high.

"She's not *fresh pussy*," I bite out before pushing to my feet and rounding the desk. Valen stands, his face inches from mine, and my blood turns hot. "She's…"

I am not even sure what to call her. But she isn't like the other girls we bring home, have our fun with, and send packing. As much as I would love to see Brielle walk out of here and never return, I can't do it. Going back on my father's last wish would break down connections. I must be the obedient heir to the throne.

"What is she then, Jude?" Val asks me, his tone taking on a darker grit, while his gaze burns me. "Because you can't tell me you haven't noticed how beautiful she is, I know you'd be lying if you did. And you can't stop the fact you're destined to walk down the aisle and bring her into this family."

I know exactly what he means when he says *family*. It's more than the blood running through my veins. It's far more than the connections built in the organisation—he's talking about the three of us.

"Into this dynamic," I add with a nod recognising what he means.

I can't stop myself from reaching for Val's face, my fingers digging into his chin as I pull him nearer. Our lips brush against each other. I want to kiss him, but before I do, I smile. I love him, I've loved him for a very long time. With a quick glance at Kai, I arch a brow and grin. Both men are mine, as I am theirs. We have belonged together since we first felt the emotions for each other coursing through us—it just took us some time to admit to them.

Glancing back at Valen, I whisper along his lips, "She's a spy." My cock throbs when he reaches for it through my slacks. His fingers tightening, squeezing as he holds my hardening dick in his hand. My zipper becomes impossibly tight. "She needs to be dealt with in the only way we know how."

"You think she's a hidden threat?" This comes from Kai as he joins us.

He's always been the peacekeeper between Valen and me. Even though he's the one who enjoys hand to hand combat, he's more of a lover than anything else.

"I don't think we should trust her, that's all. There's nothing more to talk about now. I'm done with this back and forth. She's here to stay, so we need to weed out any information we can," I say as I step back from the guys. "We have to remember, a threat can lurk anywhere, even inside our own organisations."

I turn away, focusing my attention on the gardens. I've inherited a world that keeps us away from our adversaries, away from the life my brothers and I grew up in. But even so, there's no escape from those who want to kill us. We may be feared by many, but still there are those who want to take us down.

And that's why Brielle's father is on my radar. He offered up his daughter as if she was a sacrifice. It doesn't make sense to me. However, there's nothing we can't uncover. She may intend to keep her secrets, but they won't stay hidden for very long.

"Maybe it's because he finally wants to return," Val suggests. "I mean, he must realise his daughter could be in danger. Or maybe, while he was in London, he got himself into some trouble with the mafia there, and agreeing to give Brielle to you means he knows she'll be safe."

"True," Kai says as he turns to the window. "He could have come to the conclusion it's his only option." We stand at the window, looking out over the island. I ponder their words as I focus on what I own.

The view from my office overlooks the rest of the island. The Venier estate stands on one side of the isle, on a cliff top above the crashing waves. And the university is on the other side. From here, I can see the campus in the far distance, and nestled in the middle of the island are the dorms, houses, and shops that occupy the rest of Black Hollow.

There's an unparalleled beauty on the island.

But there's also danger—dark and foreboding.

We all finally look at each other again as the questions continue to form. There could be many answers, but one thing is for sure, Saviatti is intelligent enough to realise the only way to keep his daughter safe is to give her to me.

However, even though we try to ensure everyone who attends is loyal to the families that govern the university, people can be bought. Minds can be controlled, even when it comes to those who belong to the Cosa Nostra.

I don't think we're ever safe. Not even for a moment.

Everyone has a price.

"We will figure it out," I finally say. "In other news," I continue, hoping to change the subject from the girl who has been the only thought in my mind since I first laid my eyes on her. "We need to get the new professors brought in for interviews. They've all come highly recommended from Rome."

I make my way to the desk, and settling in my chair, I pull out the three folders I received a few days ago. Before Brielle and the contract, I had work to focus on. Since her, I've become distracted.

"Do you want us in on the meetings?" Valen asks.

"No, I'll talk to them. I want you both watching her. I know you're teaching classes this afternoon, but I'd like you to each take a shift. No matter the reason for her father wanting her here, we know there will be a threat to her safety."

"You seem very concerned about protecting her." Kai's tone changes, it's now filled with intrigue as he crosses his arms and regards me with a stare that looks right through me.

I pin him with a glare. Not because he's angered me, but because I don't want to respond to him. There's no reason, at least not one I'm willing to admit to, for me to want to protect her. Other than the fact she's a possession, and I always take care of my property.

But Kai thinks there's more to it—I can read it in the glint of his eye.

"Hey, don't blast the messenger," Kai responds. "It's just an observation. There's nothing wrong with wanting to keep her safe. Fuck it, I'm more than willing to keep her right by my side all day, every day."

"That's because you want to fuck her," Val throws out, and they both laugh.

I'm not amused at all. I fist my hands on the desk before taking a deep breath.

"I can't deny she's beautiful," I finally reply after I've calmed myself. "But, I don't trust anyone until they've proven themselves. As you both know."

These guys have been around me all my life. We have grown up together and have learnt each other's strengths and weaknesses. They've seen me at my best and my worst. They know what I'm like when I am focused. When all that matters is making someone pay.

"It's not going to be easy to bring her into the dynamic, but it can be done. Perhaps she needs to have some time-out in the dungeon, let's see how strong she really is," Kai tells me as he settles on the sofa, one leg crossed over the other. "But it's a decision we all make together. Frankly, I would love to see how she deals with that."

The idea of having Brielle down there is intriguing. "What do you think?" I look at Valen.

"If she can deal with it, then we'll know she's strong. And having her on our side will ensure she's loyal when the time comes." He looks at me, his response has me nodding.

"Perhaps we find the right moment to do it. I think we need to instil a bit of fear in her, just to see if she breaks," I say as I consider watching her come into her own. I don't think she'll break, but the thought is intoxicating to say the least.

"She'll have to learn about everything," Kai says. "I'll gladly train her. Make sure she's ready for whatever comes her way."

"Good," I respond with a nod. "Let's get to work. I'm meeting with the new professors soon. They should be flying in shortly, and once those interviews are over, we can figure out what to do with the new princess."

"And she certainly is a princess," Valen remarks, causing me to flick my gaze his way.

He's clearly entranced with her. I think we all are, but there is one hurdle to overcome before we can even consider allowing her in—she needs to make her first kill. And once she does that, we will have the leverage we need to keep her right here.

She will be our queen.

TWISTED PROMISES

BRIELLE

I'VE MANAGED TO AVOID JUDAH AS MY FIRST WEEK OF studying comes to an end. I didn't want to be here, but after attending classes, and finding kinship with the small handful of girls who are studying here, I've settled into a routine—wake up, get out of the house, and spend the day at university. When I do return in the early evenings, it's quiet.

But it's finally come time to talk to Emilio. Even though he's my half-brother and we've been civil, I haven't been able to bring myself to say much more than a *good morning* to him. He looks so much like our father, it's quite disconcerting.

Saturday morning is bright. The sun is already rising when I make my way down to the kitchen. There's a handful of staff always on-site, and when I step into the warmth of the heart of the house, I find the cook busy at the hob.

She glances at me and smiles.

"Good morning, principessa," she greets me with a nod.

I still can't get used to someone calling me that. I know I'm born to a mafia family, which make me a principessa, but I grew up outside this world.

"Good morning," I respond before finding a cup and pouring some already brewed coffee.

The scent of the dark liquid makes me hum with appreciation. I add milk and settle at the table where the stack of newspapers awaits the guys. Even though we're on an island, there's still a need to keep in touch with what's happening in the outside world. It could be done via computer, but for some reason, Judah always has these papers delivered.

When I feel a presence enter the kitchen, I don't want to look, but my gaze is magnetised to the familiar man who saunters into the room. Judah is tall. His lean yet muscled body is encased in a tailored suit, perfectly fitted to his frame. The dark material against his olive skin makes him look like an Adonis. A model stepping off a runway. There's no doubt about it, he's breathtakingly gorgeous, but that doesn't stop him from being an arsehole.

Once he has his coffee in hand, he turns and seems almost surprised to see me. He doesn't greet me, he doesn't even acknowledge me as he sits across from me at the table. I watch him intently as he picks up a newspaper, flicks to a page, scans it, then sets it down.

"Today you'll go to the mainland with Valen," he says finally, then pierces me with hazel eyes. There are tiny hints of olive green in the irises, making for an intoxicating view.

"What am I meant to do there?" I lean back in my chair as I regard him.

I'm not going to allow myself to be pushed around. As much as Judah intimidates me, I'm not going to show weakness. Papa always taught me that our enemies want to discover what causes us to cower. They'll use whatever they can to see us break. Judah will learn, though, I'm not easily broken.

"You have a wedding to plan," he announces as he pushes to his feet. It's the last thing I expected him to say. "Aren't women into that kind of thing?"

His dark brow arches but is obscured by the chocolate locks hanging over his forehead. I hate that he's so beautiful to look at.

"Some women are, yes," I answer as I stand, but even as I straighten, I'm no match for him. I reach his chest at best. "But that's when they're in love with their husband-to-be," I throw out as I pin him with a glare.

"Marriage doesn't always equal love." The corners of his lips quirk up into a smirk as he looks down at me. "And vows don't always need to bring emotion. In our world, a twisted promise is as important as a vow gushed with love and devotion."

I fold my arms across my chest, and tip my chin up. "So you'd be happy with a wife you don't love, who you never touch or kiss, who you never—"

Judah leans in close causing my words get stuck in my throat as I inhale his woody cologne.

"I don't need a wife to give me anything, including a fuck," he sneers as he glares at me. "I can have a woman in my bed with a snap of my fingers. And love," he whispers now, his voice low, barely audible, "is a wasted emotion that brings pain and anguish. I don't want it or need it."

My mouth pops open but I can't find a response. My head is spinning from his admission and the masculine scent of him. He straightens easily, making sure his suit jacket is neat before he spins on his heel and heads out of the kitchen. My hands are shaking as I reach for the edge of the table.

Suddenly, the back door opens and Valen stumbles through with three large black dogs on leashes. I didn't realise there were any animals on the property—besides Judah of course.

"Hey," Valen says as his eyes land on me. "What's wrong?" Concern creases his eyebrows as he regards me with worry in his expression.

I must look like I've seen a ghost. That's what

Judah does to me, he breaks me down into tiny morsels, making it easier to devour me.

"Nothing," I tell Valen. "Well, we're going to London today as you know. I must play the happy fiancé." The harsh tone of my voice must make it clear I'm struggling with everything because Valen stares at me, waiting for me to say more.

I can't bring myself to speak, so I turn away, ignoring his stare as I refill my mug and take a long sip. The kitchen is so silent, even with the three dogs Valen's still holding. When I don't continue talking, he shrugs and gets them to sit before unleashing them. Then, they're out the door and into the garden at the back of the house.

"Are you ready to head out?" he asks as he joins me at the kitchen counter. "I just need to shower and change." I glance at him, and when he leans in close, my breath is caught in my lungs. He's handsome, breathtakingly so, and even though I'm not sure what Judah would do if he walked in right now, I can't pull away.

"I'll be ready when you are." I offer him a smile, but he doesn't seem convinced that I'm not freaked out.

I'm not sure how I feel. Perhaps it's more anger than anything else. I don't want Judah to have this effect on me, but he does. It's the cold, calculated stare he gives that sets me on edge.

"Meet you on the porch," Valen says as he leaves me in the kitchen.

Once I'm alone, I ponder my interactions with the Princes of Black Hollow, so far. Valen has been the friendliest. He's always polite and doesn't give off a threatening vibe. Though, that doesn't completely put me at ease, because these men are trained to be killers. They're practiced in the art of putting on a mask.

Kai has been elusive, for the most part, but there's something calming about him. Silent, but more than likely, deadly. All three of them are heartthrobs. But each of them very different in their demeanour and looks.

Valen has broad shoulders and a tapered waist. His body is toned and inked beautifully, which is obvious when he's wearing a T-shirt, and I can't deny I'm attracted to him. It makes me feel guilty because I'm meant to be Judah's.

Kai is the total opposite. He's bulkier in his build, with bigger muscle, I can tell he enjoys lifting weights. With shoulders that seem to fill out his shirts and tees perfectly, and at times, the material seems to strain against his body. The ink that adorns his tanned skin makes him look like a walking canvas. Whereas Valen's tattoos don't hide too much of his smooth, olive flesh.

And then there's Judah, who seems to be coiled so

tight, he's a mix between Val and Malachi. I don't know what's going to happen to me while living here, but what I do believe is that these men would do anything to protect me. I'm a possession to them, which on one hand, I hate, and on the other, I'm thankful for.

All three men have jaw bones that would make Michelangelo weep. Perfectly sculpted, with hints of dark shadow when they haven't shaved. And deep down, I realise I'm helplessly attracted to each of them for very different reasons.

I finish my coffee and head back to my bedroom where I change into a pair of black, skinny jeans and a blush pink, long-sleeved jumper that's loose and baggy. Slipping my feet into a pair of black boots, I zip them up on the side then quickly tie my hair into a messy bun. I'm not going out on a date, I'm not here to impress anyone, so this will do.

I grab my phone, which is pointless because the only person I want to contact is Papa, and I can't. When he brought me to Italy, he told me I wasn't to call or text. Instead, he would be in touch when he could. I can't help but worry about him. He's been my rock since I was a child. He saved me from this life, and even though he's thrown me back into the lion's den, I can't hate him for it.

I know there's so much more to this arrangement than meets the eye. And I intend to learn what I can.

I'll train at Black Hollow, and when the time is right, I'll leave. Judah doesn't want me here, so if I choose freedom over a loveless marriage, I'm sure he wouldn't refuse me.

I find Valen at the entrance to the house, and he smiles when his gaze lands on me. He's cute when he smiles with his dimples showing. He's wearing a short-sleeved T-shirt, which offers me a glimpse of the taut muscle in his forearms. There's a tattoo on his upper arm that I can't make out, because it's partly covered by the material, and I wonder what it is.

"Ready?" he asks, stealing my attention away from his ink, and I nod. "Let's go."

He doesn't wait for me. He opens the door and saunters out into the courtyard where one of the staff brings his car round. The sleek, matte black Maserati is beautiful. On the front of the car is a badge depicting a crown that glints in gold. It's the symbol I've seen on the bedroom doors of the Princes.

Valen gets in the driver's side while I slip into the passenger seat beside him. I'm immediately impressed at how soft the leather interior feels. I grew up in a small town in the English countryside, far away from prying eyes. But when we moved to London, there were some kids at school who had this kind of luxury, but I didn't. Papa said he didn't want us to live a lavish lifestyle, and instead, my old beat-up Ford was my first and only car.

Valen pulls out of the driveway so fast, the tyres squeal on the gravel, and we head off towards the airstrip where I landed a week ago.

"Are you enjoying Black Hollow?" Valen asks as he quickly glances over at me before turning his attention back to the road.

"It's…" I'm not sure what to call it, so I opt for, "It's interesting."

"How are your classes?"

I smile when I recall how much I love my Philosophy and History classes.

"They're better than I imagined. I'm enjoying them. I didn't expect the students to be as focused as they are. It's refreshing to see. When I was at school, there were so many kids who just wanted to do the minimum necessary to get by. Here it seems exams and tests are welcomed."

"The university is elite," Valen tells me. "When Judah hires the professors, he vets them, and they go through several interviews before they're employed to make sure they are the very best in their field. We also have to be careful as there are many enemies who want a chance to get onto the island."

This startles me. "So, even here, you're not free from threat?" I keep my focus on him, on his profile, and I can't stop myself from admiring his cut jawline.

His smooth tanned skin looks so soft, I almost want to reach out and touch it.

"Of course," Valen answers as he flicks his eyes over to me. "We're the next Bosses of our families. There will always be a threat hanging over us. We may demand respect and loyalty, but it's not always given."

I wonder if it's the reason my father didn't want me to live with him when he returned to Italy. Granted, the threat on his life is far greater because he broke the rule of omertà. However, if something happens to him, I'm the only surviving kin of the Saviatti family. But as I slot the pieces into place, trying to figure it out, I realise I'm not the next in line for my father's throne, Emilio is.

"So, Emilio—"

"He would take over your family's organisation if anything happened to your father," Valen finishes my thought. "I know you don't know him and didn't grow up with him, but he's a good guy."

"I think I was more surprised that my father didn't ever mention him. It's not like he didn't have the opportunity my entire life."

We pull into the hangar, and Valen kills the engine.

"Don't be too hard on your father. I know he's not the most respected man among the families, but he did what was needed to keep you safe. That's good in my eyes. He could have done it in a better way, but none of us are perfect."

I glance up at Valen, and his gaze pierces me. I note his eyes are similar to Judah's, but there's a hint more green in them than in his best friend's.

"I think Judah is of the opinion that he's more than perfect."

This causes Valen to laugh out loud. "Judah is a good guy. I've known him my entire life. He may come across as an arsehole, but I respect him. He would do anything for those he cares about. He may not let someone in easily," he says as he pushes his car door open before glancing at me from over his shoulder. "But once he does, you will never doubt his feelings."

"I won't hold my breath while waiting for him to ever accept me into his life."

After we exit the vehicle, Valen steps up beside me, and taking my hand, he looks directly into my eyes. It's as if he's looking for answers I'm not sure I have.

"Don't give up on him, please. There's a lot more to him than you think, and…" His voice trickles off into silence, for a moment, before he continues, "Please, give him time." It's a strange request, especially coming from Valen. It makes me wonder just how much of Judah's personality is hiding under the cold exterior. And also, why Valen is so adamant that I give his best friend a chance. "He is a good person. And once you're allowed into his world, there's no leaving. Loving him isn't easy, but it's worth the hard work to get there. And there is a lot more to this than meets the eye."

My brows furrow as I regard him with confusion. "What do you mean?"

"Let's go," he says, instead of answering my question.

I follow close behind Valen, wanting to know what he meant, but the moment we reach the aircraft, we're met by the cabin staff, guards, and the pilot who offers Valen a greeting that indicates respect, but I can tell from how he looks at Val, there is knowing behind it. He is aware of just *who* Valen is.

The Princes will soon become Kings. They'll rule, and anyone who isn't on board or doesn't offer them loyalty and respect will be ruthlessly dealt with. The mafia don't mess around when it comes to the laws they live by. I know how this life works.

When we're seated, a hostess brings me an orange juice, while Valen has a beer set in front of him.

"Are you going to answer me?" I question the moment we have privacy.

"You'll find out everything in good time, sweetheart," he tells me as the corner of his mouth tilts upward. "Are you looking forward to doing some shopping today?"

His change of subject sets me on edge, but I don't push it. I won't, not until I have to. For now, I'm going to spend the day far from Judah, which is exactly what I need.

"I am."

Even though it's for a wedding I don't want, I know that at least I'll be safe under Judah's protection. If only for a short while.

A PRINCESS'S HEART

VALEN

I SHOULD BE ANNOYED I'VE BEEN PUT ON BABYSITTING duty, but I can't deny that watching Brie in her element is nothing short of amazing. She's alluring as she smiles and laughs with the shop assistants. And each person who comes face to face with her seems to be enamoured by her beauty.

She's long since loosened her hair that now hangs in soft waves down the middle of her back. Her cheeks are rosy, blushed by the sunlight as we walk down a very busy Regent's Street. Each boutique we enter makes her glimmer with excitement. She's like a fucking star in the night sky. One that I didn't know I wanted to see, but now I'm blinded by her beauty.

As she disappears into another changing room, I pull out my phone and type out a message to Judah. We're going to have to sit her down and talk to her. Even though he doesn't trust her, we have no choice but to keep her in our lives now. There are things we need to learn about her, and she about us, and the sooner we explain our dynamic to her, the easier things will be.

She has to marry Judah, there's no doubt about it, which means she's going to have to come to terms with how we live our lives. I've a feeling that could go either way.

Brielle is going to need to learn to be shared. She'll have to come to terms with having three men who want her, desire her, and will have her. She has no choice in her husband, but she will also have two other men who are about to become part of her life. The dynamic we have is strong, and I am sure adding her to it will only strengthen us. As long as Judah can ease his worry about her intentions and reasons for being here.

My phone buzzes as she exits the changing room. The dress she's wearing won't go down well with Judah, but I'm not going to deny the chance to see her in it again. The long flowing material hugs every curve of her body. She's got the perfect hourglass shape, and the deep cut in the front offers up a glimpse of her cleavage. This is why women make better spies than men do—they're able to distract with a sway of their hips or a pout of their lips. And I would go down without a fight if there was a beautiful woman capturing my attention.

Maybe it's a weakness, but I'll die happy if I have to.

"Is this okay?" She looks down at herself as she speaks, then glances into the mirror, taking in her reflection.

There's a shyness to Brielle, an uncertainty that she's up to standard. Perhaps she wasn't when she lived in England, but on Black Hollow, she's going to be the belle of the ball.

"I would say so," I manage to utter as she looks over to me, waiting on my answer. "I think perhaps you need a higher heel with that one, but the colour looks perfect on you."

It's not a lie. The deep navy blue against her tanned skin makes her look like the princess she is. Her long, dark hair hangs in waves, and when she turns around again, I realise the dress will cause an uproar in the house. There's no back at all. At least not very much of one.

The thought of Judah losing his shit makes me chuckle. Brielle glances at me from over her shoulder. The siren within our midst, the one who'll send us all to our death with a mere glimmer in those pretty eyes.

"What?" she asks as she stares at me.

I can read the uncertainty in her stance. It's something Judah would enjoy. He has a commanding presence, and he loves making girls squirm under his intense scrutiny. But also, this is his future wife, so it may be more of a game to him than any of the other females he's had in his bed.

"Nothing," I tell her with a shake of my head. "It's perfect."

She disappears from sight, and I open the message from Judah. He's calling a meeting this evening. All five of us will need to be in attendance, which means he has a plan he'd like to pursue. Or he's found out more about our little princess.

"I'm done. We can go home now. I'm tired of playing dress up." Her voice catches my attention, and she's once more dressed in her jeans and sweater.

Her curves are now hidden from prying eyes. Mine. But for a moment, I can't help but recall how she looked in the dresses she's tried on today, especially the last one—the meagre material barely hiding her luscious body. It was a dress made for a trained killer. One that could have you rock hard, just before she slits your throat. And I'd be lying if I said it didn't turn me the fuck on. I'd love to watch her do just that, see her in her element. Because soon she's going to realise who she is—the future Queen of the Venier family.

"We should get back to the island," I tell her as I push to my feet.

It's going to be a long afternoon and evening,

and I'm pretty sure Judah is going to want a rundown on everything she said. There wasn't much that made me think she's spying on us, though.

Our talks have been mostly about her studies. She's intelligent, fiery, and fascinating. She doesn't show an interest in any of the male students at the university, at least she hasn't mentioned any. She seems to mostly keep to herself, which is welcome. Having to keep an eye on her twenty-four-seven would be difficult, so Brielle's aloneness is most definitely helpful. The one good thing, is that Brielle doesn't appear to know about our pasts. Some things should never see the light of day.

However, secrets rarely stay buried. They eventually find a way to come to light, and when that happens, it tends to blow up. Especially when it comes to Judah, Kai, and me.

Once I pay the bill, we head back to the car park in silence. But the moment we slip into the backseat of the limo, it's Brielle who says, "I want to know what's going on between you, Kai, and Judah."

"What?" I snap my gaze to hers.

I wasn't expecting her to say that, and I have to tread carefully because there are things she may freak out about. I can't let that happen.

"I saw you and Kai with that girl," Brielle says, but she doesn't meet my gaze.

Her cheeks darken to a deep pink, and I'm pretty sure they'd be bright red if I divulged all our secrets.

"Yeah," I respond, wary of taking it too far.

This time, Brielle does look my way. "You were… both of you…" She stumbles over her words, and as predicted, those cheeks of hers darken.

"We were both fucking her," I say with a shrug. "Haven't you ever heard of a threesome?"

The thought of having Brielle between us, including Judah, does something to me. I recognised her beauty the moment she came into view. When I first laid eyes on her, I was entranced by her, and the image of her naked, in the throes of passion, with our hands all over her and cocks inside her has me stifling a groan.

"I have," Brielle retorts, folding her arms across her chest. "I just wanted to know if all three of you do that. You're very close and seem to be much more than just friends."

"You've noticed that?" I question as I arch a brow at her.

"Well, there's something between you three," she says, shrugging. "Maybe I'm seeing things or reading too much into it."

She turns away, and I can't help but smile. It's always been obvious to those close to us we're more than just friends. There are those small touches, those long stares between us. Occasionally, Jordan has walked in on a kiss that perhaps shouldn't have happened. But Judah's brother has known about our unconventional relationship for years, and he's never judged.

I came to the conclusion I was bisexual when I was in my early teens, and I started to look at Judah in a different light. I saw more than just my best friend. It was only once we'd moved to Black Hollow that the connection grew. The same with Malachi. Our relationship wouldn't be acceptable to our parents—they're strait-laced in their views, which means we have to be careful while we're still awaiting the moment to step into our roles as head of our organisations. If anyone found out before we're made Bosses, before we're given the keys to our respective kingdoms, all hell would break loose.

"Some things aren't spoken about in public, princess," I finally offer her an answer.

Even though our drivers are trusted, we have to be careful. We're so close to claiming our organisations, and we don't want anything to get in the way.

For the rest of the journey home, I manage to avoid any more questions about the relationship between me, Kai, and Judah. When we walk into the house, it's a hive of activity.

Jordan spots us as he comes down the stairs.

"Princess," he says with a smile, and I notice how receptive and friendly Brielle is with him.

It's a different story when it comes to Judah, but then again, my best friend isn't the warmest of people around strangers. There have been times women have run out here petrified after he's lost his shit. Which, to be fair, is quite funny to watch from the sidelines. The thing about Judah is that he doesn't take shit. He is upfront and open about his feelings. And it's not always a good thing, especially when you're not used to his arsehole ways.

"Did you have a good day?" Jordan asks as he beams at Brielle.

"Yeah, it wasn't too bad actually. Valen isn't the worst company in the world," she jokes, and the soft giggle that escapes her lips has me grinning.

"I'm charming and alluring," I counter as I pass by her and drop my keys on the table that sits just to the side of the front door.

"Go to your bedroom, Brielle," Judah says, having appeared from the hallway where the offices are located.

Within the mansion, we've set up three offices, one for each of us—mine, Kai's, and Judah's. It's where we're able to work in privacy. Even though our families are loyal to one another, they all have their own secrets, and they expect us to keep them. Our separate offices give an appearance of secrecy, but the thing is, we don't follow the rules. We have broken down the barriers that keep us separate, and between the three of us, there are no secrets. We believe that what our families don't know, won't get us into shit. That's how it's always been between us, and I doubt it will ever change.

"I'm not a child."

"I don't give a shit what you are or what you're not. I'm telling you to go to your room. We have things to discuss, and I don't need a little spy running around the house."

Brielle's anger is clear as she leans up into Judah's face. For a moment, I see the flicker of desire between them. It appears she has a crush on him. I don't blame her—he's beautiful. But what surprises me is the need in his eyes. He finds her alluring.

"I'm. Not. A. Child." She annunciates each word slowly. "Don't ever talk to me like that again."

When she takes a step backwards, Judah's hand shoots out quickly to grip her wrist. I know this isn't going to end well, and I want nothing more than to stop them, but I also know they need to work through their issues. I place a hand on his shoulder, but his frustration is taking hold. He tightens his grip and drags her behind him up the staircase, his long strides causing Brielle to stumble as she struggles to keep up.

"Jude," I call to him as they reach the top of the stairs.

"Meet me in the office, Val," is his only response.

I know there's no arguing with Judah when he's in this mood, so I watch him and Brielle disappear, but not before she glances my way, and for a moment, I want to run to her. I can't explain it, but there's a protective need that courses through me. One I haven't felt before.

"You know he's obsessed with her," Jordan says as he and Kai join me.

The younger Venier brother is a couple of years our junior, but he's been brought into the family business because his father wanted it. None of us have a choice, but at least our fate isn't as bad as my sister's, who will be sent off to marry someone of my father's choosing.

The inequality angers me, but there's nothing we can do about it. Not until we take over and can change the rules. Why should women be overlooked and used as pawns. They have strengths and skills that the men in our world could never possess.

"I know he is," I tell him as I shake my head.

The thing is, Judah won't accept it until it slaps him in the face. And by then, she may have already made her mind up about him.

"I doubt he's ever going to trust her," Kai adds.

I look at him and smile. "There are many times

I've thought one thing and Judah's done the exact opposite. For now, I think he wants to suss her out more than anything. She will marry him, and he's going to have to accept it," I say. "As time goes by, he'll come to realise not everyone wants to kill him."

Kai's gaze flicks to mine. "What if she is a spy?"

I glance at him for a long moment. "Honestly? I'm not sure. I know that Judah will never stand for it."

"Do you think he'd actually kill her?" Jordan asks.

I'm not sure how to answer his question. We've never had to interrogate a female before. Under our rule, all those who've broken the code have been men. But that's mostly because women aren't allowed in the organisations.

"I don't know," I reply as we make our way to the office.

If we discover Brielle's betrayed us, I know it won't be easy for us to bring her into the dungeon for interrogation. She's a beautiful young woman. We've never once hurt a female, and I'm certain we never intend to. Which means that Judah may go after her father as payback for any betrayal.

"Her father could become the target, instead," Jordan says, voicing my thoughts.

"He could, and it would make life a lot easier," I respond as the three of us settle into seats around the table. The round, mahogany surface is gleaming, which means the office has been cleaned. "I wonder if it's been polished," I think out loud.

"It has," Jordan confirms. "You know," he continues, his voice taking on a hushed whisper. "Judah was in the girl's room earlier, looking for something. I'm not sure he found anything, but perhaps there's a reason she was sent here, one we haven't figured out yet."

I glance at him. "What makes you say that?"

Jordan shrugs, "Dunno. I guess I'm more like Judah than I thought. Trust is earned, and she hasn't done that yet."

I lean back as I ponder Jordan's words. I don't believe she's working undercover. There's far too much innocence in her eyes. I've met many traitors in my life, even though I'm only twenty-four. I've come across spies who work undercover in all sorts of organisations, and none of them have the glimmer of purity that Brielle has.

Perhaps it's time we dirtied her up.

FIGHTING BACK

BRIELLE

When we reach my bedroom, I'm pushed through the doorway and into the large space behind. I wanted nothing more than to be alone, hidden away from Judah's stare. Even though he's beautiful to look at, I know the devil was an angel too. And no matter how much of an Adonis this man before me is, he's still a monster under the tailored suits and the chiselled jawbone.

"What the hell is your problem?" I go into the attack.

"When I ask you to do something, Brielle, I expect you to obey. I don't want to repeat myself, and I don't need you putting yourself in harm's way. There are reasons for everything I do, and having you sass me at every turn isn't helping matters."

Frustration ebbs through me and flows out between us. There's no denying the electric current

135

sparking in the room, but I fight my wayward thoughts at every turn. I do not want to feel anything for Judah. I don't care how much I find him attractive.

"I'm not a child to be sent to my room when you're in a bad mood," I throw back as I spin on my heel and walk to the window. I can't look at him, because if I do, I'll end up distracted by his perfect lips, or his sharp features, or the way his eyes shimmer when he glares at me.

Even in his anger, he looks like a perfectly created statue.

"I don't give a shit what you think, or don't think, you are," Judah grits through clenched teeth. I watch the tick in his jaw as he closes the distance between us. "This life, this island, is filled with threats."

"I'm a big girl, I can take care of myself," I whisper, the heat of my confidence causing my tone to deepen. "I've lived—"

"You haven't lived in my world for very long, Brielle. You don't understand what could happen to you. I have many enemies, and if they hurt you…" His words falter for a moment, and the silence eats its way between us.

"Do… Do you care about me?" The moment the question falls from my lips, I want to drag it back in. It's stupid to think he gives a shit about me. There must be more to it than him feeling any sort of affection for me.

"I don't need innocent blood spilled in my home. There's enough on my hands," he says, stepping back suddenly as if I've slapped him. "Just obey, and we won't have any issues."

"Look at me," I order him, unable to keep myself from fighting back.

I know I have to be careful because I don't want to appear too strong while living with the Princes. I want them to underestimate me. Judah's right, this world is very different to the one I grew up in. I'm not disputing that at all. But I am more than capable of taking care of myself.

Judah spins on his heel, his eyes blazing with fury. "Never," he says as he takes a step towards me, "ever think I won't kill you."

His words have a dark promise to them. There's no doubt this man would willingly snap my neck if I gave him reason to. It doesn't matter that I'm meant to marry the bastard. He doesn't care, which means he can't ever love me.

Suddenly, without warning, tears sting my eyes when the realisation hits me square in the face. I swallow back the lump in my throat as I look up at him.

"I am exactly the bastard you think I am," Judah tells me as he grips my cheeks, causing my lips to pout. "I like seeing those tears," he admits with a glance at my eyes. "And I intend to see them often. You'll have them streaming down your cheeks on our wedding night when you finally learn the truth. You may have said *I do* to me, but you belong to all of us —you're mine, Valen's, and Kai's. Every night after we'll share what we own. And make no mistake, Brielle, you may be a gentle princess right now, but soon you'll become a cold-hearted queen, just like your kings. Anything that happens between the two of us," he says as he leans in close, "includes them as well."

He pushes me away and I stumble backwards into the wall, but he doesn't cast me another glance as he makes his way out of my room. When the door clicks shut, I half expect him to have locked me in, but when I try the handle, I realise it still opens.

I shut myself in and settle on the bed. Where Judah's fingers held me, it still tingles from his touch. It's stupid to even consider a future where we could be happy. I know he'll never love me. *But would he allow me to be with someone else?* Valen is handsome and sweet, and he treats me as an equal. The problem is, he's Judah's best friend, and I wasn't given to Valen or Kai. I was gifted to the leader of the pack.

Sighing, I lie back on the bed and stare up at the ornate ceiling. Thoughts race through my mind, and I wonder if I'll ever be free again.

Born into this world, I know none of the guys have had any life beyond their families, beyond the legacy they have to uphold. It saddens me when I think about them growing up without the freedom to choose their own future.

I'd always thought I was free to decide my fate, so when Papa said he needed me to come back with him to Italy, to return to the world he'd run from, I was shocked. I haven't told the Princes the explanation that my father gave me for returning. They wouldn't understand.

As much as I'm angry with the man who raised me, I know he's only doing it to keep me safe. Even though I don't like being here, or being near Judah and his friends, I know they'll protect me—as long as I keep obeying the commands of the soon-to-be Boss of the Venier family.

Rolling my eyes, I push to my feet and head to the bathroom. Perhaps a shower will freshen me up before I go down for dinner.

The water massages my aching muscles as I lean against the tiles. I close my eyes and allow the spray to drench me. Slowly, I lather up, but the more I run my fingertips over my skin, the more I can't get Valen out of my mind, and as much as I want to fight it, Judah appears too easily, and my hands become his hands.

Biting my lower lip, I fight the urge to moan as

pleasure skitters down my spine. My knees are weakened by the desire coursing through me. I can easily recall Valen's gaze on me today. When I think about how he watched me, taking in every outfit I modelled for him, I know without a doubt he's attracted to me.

But then, it's thoughts of Judah's touch that send heat racing between my thighs, and I can't stop my fingertips from brushing over my clit. I'm wet, and it's not only from the shower. The warmth of the water caressing my skin, along with the light touch against my pussy, sends me reeling as I grip my throat with my free hand and squeeze, ever so gently. It's not me, though. In my mind's eye, it's Judah holding me hostage while Valen drops to his knees and kisses between my thighs before his mouth captures my wetness and he laps at me. And, in the background, there's a glimpse of Kai's handsome face as he watches the display.

My knees go weak when I imagine all three men watching me. All of them staring with desire dancing in their eyes, and I can't hold back the pleasure that takes over. I whimper as I tremble, and my orgasm shatters through me, causing me to cry out.

As my hand slows, and my eyes flutter open, I half expect them to be standing at the door, watching me, but the bathroom is empty, filled instead with steam from the hot shower.

I quickly turn off the spray and step out onto the fluffy mat. Wrapped in a towel, I make my way into my empty bedroom and sigh with relief. No one heard me. I dress quickly, ignoring the reality of what I just did.

Earlier, when Judah mentioned something about me being owned by Val and Kai as well as him, my mind was a mess at the time, but since then I've run through all the scenarios of what it could mean. The only thing I can come up with is that they intend to share me. All of them.

But Malachi hasn't spent any time with me. Since I've been here, Valen is the one who's taken the lead. I wonder if he's the calmer and more approachable one. Maybe they're slowly easing me into the idea of living here, being in this world and in their lives.

The moment I walk into the living room, it's as if my fantasy has come to life. All three men are seated around the coffee table with drinks in hand. They stop talking as I step deeper into the room.

"Don't stop on my account," I say as I settle into one of the enormous armchairs.

Sinking down on the soft cushion, I suddenly feel exhausted. It's been a long day.

"Women shouldn't listen to the organisation's dealings," Judah says.

"Did you have a nice day shopping?" Kai

questions and he tips his head to the side. His eyes locked on mine.

It's one of the very few times I've really looked at him. There's a darkness in his gaze, one that promises he'd do anything for his family. Danger emanates from him in waves.

I glance between the three handsome faces. I don't know whether they can read the guilt in my expression, but if they can, they don't show it.

"I've spent my life around my father who taught me how to run a business. I managed accounts with him, learning as I went."

Anger takes over when I consider just what these arseholes think of me. I'm not going to sit back and be the helpless princess they believe I am. The thought has me rising from my seat, so I can stand and face them.

Judah leans his elbow on the arm of the sofa and rests his chin on his fingers. The side glance he offers me makes me inch back, just slightly, and I know he's noticed my movement. One thing about Judah Venier, he's perceptive.

"Sit," he orders as he arches a dark brow.

I cross my arms in front of me and pin him with a glare. The need to challenge him and fight back is coursing through my veins.

"I'm hungry," I bite out. "And I don't take orders from you."

Without responding, Judah pushes to his feet. Each movement slow and calculated. When he reaches me, he leans forward. The warmth of his breath fans over my face, and his eyes glimmer with intent.

"It seems our little princess has found a backbone." The smirk that curls his lips makes my blood run cold.

Judah reaches for me and holds me steady. That's when I feel warmth at my back. Valen and Kai have closed in. Three imposing Princes surrounding me, an almost helpless girl who they've captured in their den.

"I quite like you fighting back, little spy," Judah tells me. "It makes my cock hard," he says in a low, gravelly tone that sends a trickle of desire through me.

I want to fight my feelings for him. I want to hate him, but I can't deny just how beautiful he is. The eyes that hold my gaze hostage shine with another emotion. Alongside the anger...I see lust.

"Let me go," I mumble as Judah grips my chin.

He turns my head from left to right, and I take in the other two hunters who are now in position on either side of me. It's as if my fantasy has come to play. It's real, and I don't have anywhere to run.

"Because of your father," Judah says, "You'll never be free of us. This life is now yours forever. So, princess, I think you should forget about any romantic ideas of fairy tales and happy ever afters." Judah's tone remains serious, but there's also a hint of something I can't quite put my finger on. "Our world is made for violence, bloodshed, and torture."

Kai moves in closer, and I'm cocooned in their domineering presence.

"You will always be ours, princess," Kai tells me, and this causes me to jerk my head from Judah's hold because these are the first words Kai has spoken to me directly, and I glare at him.

I keep being told I'm theirs, but it makes no sense. I'm promised to Judah.

"You all keep saying that you own me, but what does it actually mean?" I question. "Because I'm not some possession you can all toy with."

Kai glances at Judah, something silent passes between them. Then I notice how his stare flicks to the person on the other side of me, Valen. They're keeping a secret, one I have to learn because I'm not going to stay in the dark while they're messing with my head. It's time I fight back, just like Papa taught me.

"It's time to tell the princess," Valen says, and I snap my gaze to his from over my shoulder.

He looks at me, but there isn't any malevolence in his eyes, not like Judah's. That's what I find so strange about the three of them. They're all so different in their personalities, but they're such close friends.

Even though this life comes with the promise of loyalty, not every friend remains true. At least, that's what I've learnt over the years. Jealousy can come in many forms, and most of the time, it's those who are the closest that will take a shot, just to get whatever it is they want.

"I'm not leaving this room until one of you tells me what's going on," I grit through clenched teeth, frustration finally taking its toll on me.

I can't do this anymore. My father kept secrets from me all my life, he even had a son I didn't know about. I'm done with things hidden in the dark because they always come to light, and usually at the most inopportune times.

Kai takes a step towards Judah, and Valen's hand slips around me as he pulls me closer. It's then that a gasp of surprise slams right into my chest when Judah and Kai's lips meet in a gentle yet passionate kiss.

Valen's lips brush against my ear, causing warmth to course through my veins.

"There are secrets in this house, that need to stay behind closed doors, princess," he whispers as we watch the two men kissing.

Never in my life did I imagine I would witness

this, but I can't deny, there's something erotic and sensual about their union.

When they finally break the kiss, Judah nods at Kai who then turns towards me. Kai cups my face in his hands, and he leans in. Even as his lips brush against mine, my stare is on Judah. But he doesn't stop us when Kai kisses me. His tongue dances along my lips, and I can't help but open my mouth, allowing him inside. He's gentle and passionate.

Then, Valen's hands reach up in front of me, and he cups my breasts so lovingly I tremble. His fingers tweak my nipples, causing me to whimper into the kiss.

When the men step back, I'm left shivering and cold from the loss of their warm presence, and I can't find words to explain what's racing through my mind.

"That, princess," Kai says as he regards my shocked features, "is what we mean."

When Judah steps towards me once more, his hand grips my face, squeezing my cheeks so I can't move. His eyes blaze with fire.

"I'll only say this once," he tells me, keeping his voice low. "If this ever gets out, then it will be on you."

The underlying threat is clear. I can't tell anyone about what I've seen between them.

He releases me, and I can't help myself from

saying, "You may think I'm a spy, but I'm not. I don't go around telling everyone things that aren't mine to tell. If you want to live in the shadows, that's on you," I say as I prod at Judah's chest. It's the equivalent of poking a sleeping bear. "But in this day and age, no one gives a shit."

"Our fathers' do," Valen says, and Judah flinches. His father is dead. It's the first time I've seen any sort of emotion on his face, other than rage and anger. "We could lose everything if they found out. They still have those old school ideals, and what we have between us is wrong in their eyes."

If I'm being honest, I didn't think about it like that. I know how certain relationships cause tension amongst families. Parents who refuse to accept something they don't understand. Perhaps that's why Judah has been so adamant in keeping me at arm's length. But now, he has no reason to. Knowing they're happy, they're in love, makes this a beautiful situation rather than a dynamic that should be judged. They're not hurting each other—they're keeping each other safe, loved.

"Well," I respond, turning to Valen and Kai. "I'm not going to say anything." Relief washes over both of them. It's the truth, though. Theirs is not a conventional relationship by any means, but I've come to like Valen, he's a good person. I don't know Kai so well, but there's a quiet calm that follows him.

The only person in this room that could be an issue for me is the man I'm going to marry.

And then it's Kai who says, "So now you understand what this means for you. There never only be two of you in the marriage. It will be all of us."

POSSESSIVE PRINCES

KAI

I'M NOT AT ALL SURE WHAT SHE'S REALLY THINKING. Not many people can accept our rather unique bond, but then again, not many people know about it. But now it's a secret she'll have to carry.

We've always tried to keep our connection private. If anyone from the families finds out about us, it would mean our downfall. We would lose our rightful places as heirs. I never want to lose Judah and Val, but I don't want to step away from the head of the Errani family either.

"I... I..." It's clear Brielle is in shock, but she hasn't run away, that's a bonus. "I don't know what to say."

"Well," Judah starts, and I pray he doesn't say something to scare the princess off. "This is our life. We've lived this way since we were seventeen. Nothing has changed it, and nothing will."

His ultimatum is clear. Judah isn't going to alter his lifestyle for anyone, not even his future wife. We don't know Brielle, and he's right that she could be a spy, but I think we have to give her the benefit of the doubt.

"I'd never ask you to change," Brielle says, her cheeks are flushed and her lips pouty, making my cock ache.

When I realised I was bi, I didn't think anything of it. I am attracted to both men and women. But I've always known it would never be accepted in the family. Not by my mother or my father. And losing my inheritance is something I can't risk.

"We need you to understand this is the biggest secret you'll ever keep," I tell Brielle, taking a step closer to her. The sweetness of her perfume makes me fucking ache. I grip her chin, gently at first, then I tighten my fingers before lowering my hand to grasp her neck. "If anyone finds out…" a cruel smile curls my lips, "you *will* pay."

"I need time," Brielle whispers as she looks at me, and tugs away from my harsh grip. She turns her stare towards Valen before focusing her attention solely on Judah. "I'm not going to spill your secrets," she tells him. "But I need time."

"Of course," Judah answers with a nod before he turns and leaves us.

Judah isn't one for affection—he doesn't offer it

and he doesn't accept it. The man is stone cold, and he doesn't like to show emotion. I can count on one hand the number of times I've seen him lose his composure.

There's a very clear chemistry between Brielle and Judah, but it can be volatile. Mainly because he doesn't trust her. It will take time for their relationship to develop. But we all want this to work. She didn't immediately run off after our confession, so I'm hopeful, given the time, she'll be willing to accept us.

"Are you hungry?" I ask, turning my attention back to Brielle.

There's something about the little princess that makes me want to look after her, to protect her. Since she's come into our lives, she's been under our watchful eye. But now she knows our secret, it's even more important to keep her safe.

She nods with a small smile on her pretty face. "I am."

"Shall we go out for dinner?" I suggest as I glance at her and then Valen.

We can go out to the pizza place down the road. It will give us some time outside the mansion, and it may help clear Brielle's mind from worry and concern.

I haven't spent a lot of time with her. But I realise now it's been a mistake. Valen's taken the lead, and he's the one she calls on if she needs anything. But I want to be there for her too. I can't deny she's gorgeous. She makes my cock stand to attention at times, especially when she's being cheeky in her responses. The brat inside her shows up, every now and again. And I love it.

"Let's go," I say as I leave her with Valen and make my way to the door.

They follow behind, but there's no sign of Judah. I slip into the driver's seat of my SUV. Valen joins me up front, while Brielle is seated in the back. Before I start the engine, I pull out my phone and send a message to Judah. He doesn't need to know where we are all the time, and I doubt he cares, but I think if he was to join us, it may be for all our benefit.

"How are you liking the island so far," Valen asks Brielle, and I'm intrigued to hear her answer.

"It's beautiful. I didn't think I would enjoy being away from London so much, but coming from a big city, I think it's a welcome retreat in many ways."

"Good," Valen says, but I stay silent.

It's just who I am. I don't like showing my cards too soon. We've already confessed more than I'd like, but it's been necessary. She says she needs time, so we need to give her space. The main thing is she didn't run.

When I pull up to the restaurant, I kill the engine and exit the vehicle. Opening the rear passenger door, I help Brielle from the car, and I can't ignore the spark that courses through me when she touches my hand.

Inside, the restaurant is busy with students and professors from the university. It's the weekend, so I'm not surprised. Once we're seated at a table in the back corner, I take in each face. Even on the island, I know we're not safe from the threat of those who want us dead.

"Hey, guys," the waitress says with a smile as she sets the menus down.

"Two large Sicilian pizzas, two garlic breads, and three glasses of Merlot," I order without bothering to look at her.

My attention is solely on the girl who's sitting opposite me, the one who is now a part of my life.

Once we're alone again, Brielle pins me with a glare, and I have to fight back the need to laugh. Her fire is fun to play with. I've always been a fan of danger. And I certainly don't shy away from it. Especially when it's so beautiful.

"I'm able to order for myself," she throws at me, her eyes blazing with frustration. "I don't like being treated as if I'm helpless."

"I never once thought you were," I tell her as I tip my head to the side, regarding her with interest. "I just don't need to sit here for twenty minutes while you scan through the options before deciding on the one pizza that has all the toppings. One that's delicious and I know you'll enjoy."

Her glare attempts to burn me, but I don't allow it. One thing I've learnt, over the years, is to never show weakness. It gives your enemy an advantage. But if you show them you're unfazed by any threat, you'll ensure your victory.

"And how do you know I'll enjoy it?"

I can't stop the smirk that curls my lips. "Well," I start as I lean back in my seat and meet her stare directly. "As well as cheese and olives, it's topped with a variety of three sausages. What's not to love?"

Her cheeks darken to a deep red at the innuendo, and I'm proud she understood it. The wine arrives before Brielle can reply, but I've a feeling she doesn't have too much to say. She quickly picks up her drink and swallows back a mouthful. The stain on her lips makes them look even plumper than usual, and the sheen of wetness makes me throb against my zipper.

"Something I said?" I ask, arching a brow as I watch her reaction with interest.

"Not at all," Brielle replies. "So," she continues. "What do you do all day? I know Valen teaches, but what is it that you bring to the island?"

"I teach as well. However, my classes are off-site, in a private building not far from the university campus."

I pick up my drink and savour the Merlot—deep,

rich berry flavours burst on my tongue, and I wonder briefly what it would taste like trickled over the smooth, tanned skin of the woman before me.

"Kai," a voice calls to me and I glance up to see Sofia, one of the female students I had riding my dick a few weeks ago. "Are you racing tomorrow?"

I notice how she looks at Brielle with interest, and I'm fairly sure she's trying to figure out who Brielle is in relation to me.

"Maybe," I reply, but I don't look at Sofia. My focus is on the pretty princess sitting opposite me.

"I'd like to see you again, Kai." Sofia is starting to sound desperate, and it takes me a few moments before I drag my gaze over to her.

"We're done," I tell her, not giving a shit at the way her lower lip wobbles. I've never had a girlfriend, I don't do that shit, and I don't intend on making her mine.

"I thought—"

"Listen, Sofia," Valen says as he rises. "Let's talk."

He takes her by the arm and leads her away. and I'm thankful for it. I didn't want to lose my shit in front of Brielle. She'll learn who I am soon enough, but for now, I want her to enjoy her meal in peace.

The waitress brings our order over, and the fragrance of the pizza has me salivating.

I look at Brielle and say, "Eat."

"I'm not one of your fuck toys," she bites out as

she grabs a piece of the garlic bread then licks her fingers.

I want to fight this desire I feel for her, but I can't. Her lips shimmer with oil and wine. I want to lick her mouth—I want to taste her.

Clearing my throat, I shift in my seat and lean forward. "You're not one of my fuck toys, because I discard them when I'm done, but make no mistake, Brielle, you are mine."

She glowers at me as I feel a presence at our table. I turn my attention to the guy who's standing there, staring at Brielle. I recognise him instantly. He's one of the new students, an up-and-coming Boss who'll be at the university for at least the next three or four years before he's ready to take on his family's organisation. He's nothing more than a kid playing grown up games.

We haven't met before, but I have a feeling, by the way he's looking at Brielle, he's going to become well acquainted with my fist in a second.

"Can I help you?" My voice is a low, warning rumble as I glare at him.

Staring daggers at the bastard, I'm ready to attack. I haven't drawn blood in a while, and I'm feeling hungry to do just that with this little shit.

"I was just wondering if your girl here has a date for the dance." He looks at me and smiles.

He probably thinks it's worth taking a chance

because I don't have Brielle on my lap and my arm's not wrapped around her.

"How about you take a walk?" I tell him.

"I don't know anything about a dance," Brielle says at the same time I speak, and my blood warms to boiling point when she smiles at the bastard.

Before he has time to respond, I'm on my feet and in his face. I'm taller than him, and I hover close to his face before I grip his throat. My hand captures the column of very delicate bones. I could squeeze now and steal his breath. I could tighten my hold and make him see stars. And if I increase the pressure further, I could break bones that are integral to this arsehole seeing another day.

"As I said, you should take a walk. The Princes don't appreciate your bullshit," I tell him, and his eyes widen. He's realised who I am.

"K-K-Kai Errani," he mumbles.

"That's me." I smile when I feel him attempt to swallow. His Adam's apple moving against my palm. I want to choke him, to see him struggle, but instead of being a total arsehole, I release him. "Now, I trust you and your friends won't forget that this girl is off limits," I inform him only to receive a nod before he rushes past Valen who's staring at me confused.

"What the fuck was that?" he asks as he glances over his shoulder at the group of kids walking out of the restaurant.

"Arseholes," I say as I slip back into my seat.

If Brielle's glare was angry earlier, I would say right now she's livid.

"You don't own me, yet," she says. "If I want to—"

"What you want is no longer your choice. We will make sure you're safe. Don't for one second think about dating any of these kids on this island. You are owned, princess. You're ours. It doesn't matter if you want to be or not."

She pushes to her feet, but Valen is beside her in seconds.

"You don't want to fight us," he warns.

It's the first time I've seen him like this with her. Usually, he's the sweet caring one, but right now, the killer has appeared, the man who first captured my attention when I watched him torture a traitor. I knew that day I would want him in my life forever. There was something visceral about how he delved into the darkness.

He's different to Judah and me in the way he handles himself, but he's also very much like us in the way he enjoys the part of our job where rules don't matter. The three of us have a hunger for violence and a need to kill. We don't take shit from anyone, and when we do exact revenge, it's never forgotten. Which is why the Lawless Princes rule.

Valen releases Brielle's arm, and shockingly, she doesn't run, she doesn't slap him, she merely stares.

"I will make this very fucking clear to both of you, I'm here because my father wanted me to be, not because you, or you," she points at Valen then me before she continues, "or Judah have said so."

"Try to leave, and I'll find you," Judah's voice comes from behind us, causing Brielle's eyes to widen. "And you don't want to see me when I have to give chase."

It's a warning. Judah is well-equipped as a hunter, and I wouldn't want to be his prey.

Valen escorts Brielle out of the restaurant, and I ask for the pizzas to be packaged to take away. She hasn't eaten and she needs to. Perhaps it was a mistake to come out tonight, but I won't sit back and let a kid hit on the woman who belongs to us.

"What happened?"

I look at Judah as we wait for the food. "Some bastard thinks he can have what belongs to the Princes."

"Name?" Judah's voice is like ice as he speaks.

He's angry, I can read the emotion written all over his face—the fire dances in his eyes.

"Morrone, I think," I tell him, but I'm not entirely sure.

He's a new student, and I've only seen him a

couple of times. He's not advanced enough to be in my classes.

Judah nods before he leaves me staring at his back. He disappears through the doors, and I know that come tomorrow, the young bastard who tried his luck will be in the dungeon. It's an underground tunnelling system that runs the length of the island. There are small rooms every couple of miles, and that's where we take those who don't follow our rules.

As I make my way to the SUV, I can't help but wonder what the coming week will bring.

THE WAY YOU HATE

BRIELLE

I'M STILL REELING FROM THE WEEKEND. I'VE DISCOVERED secrets I never expected to learn. They probably regret what they've shared with me, but they didn't have a choice. I had to know the truth, sooner or later.

That's the thing about keeping things hidden, they always come to light. But now I need to think about the way forward. Even though I'm bound by a contract, deep down, I realise I've come to care for the Princes, even Judah. Now I know the truth, I can see why he's so distrusting of strangers, and I can't blame him. They've allowed me into their world, and confessed something I'm not sure many people know about.

Even though I'm going to become a Venier, I'm still not sure why they chose that particular moment to confess their innermost desires. In private, they're three beautiful men in an unconventional erotic relationship, but in public, they're nothing more than best friends, loyal acquaintances. It just goes to show that what you see on the outside isn't always the truth.

Black Hollow may look like paradise, but in a world filled with powerful criminals, trained in the art of deception, there are dangers lurking everywhere. And I have to remember that. All the students are the same. There's a reason they attend the university—they came here to learn how to lie and double-cross, to become the best before stepping up to their thrones.

As I walk into the university, I wonder what will happen once the wedding takes place. The guys made it clear I won't just be Judah's—I'll be owned by all three, alpha male, mafia bosses. And soon, when they take their rightful places within the families, I'll no longer just be their princess, I'll be taking on a new role as their queen.

My father never hid any secrets from me. He made sure to tell me every detail about our family business and how we came to be living in England. I grew up with knowledge I probably shouldn't have had. But I'm thankful I did learn all there was to know because it's given me an upper hand.

The classroom is already full by the time I reach it, and stepping inside, I manage to slip into an empty seat. I don't take note of the people around me, but I can feel eyes on me. It's as if they're watching, waiting for my bodyguards to arrive. With what happened at the pizza place the other night, I'm pretty sure everyone on the isle knows who I am now. And also, where I'm living.

I've always tried to stay out of the spotlight, even when I was at school in England, but with Malachi's possessive outburst, I am pretty sure I've become the talk of Black Hollow. And that puts me on edge.

Anxiety coils deep in my core, twisting in my stomach, and I have to breathe deeply and pray I don't have an anxiety attack. There have been a handful of times when I couldn't stop them, and I've ended up a mess, hiding in a corner. I know I need to focus on my breathing to keep from completely losing it now. The affliction, at least that's what I call it, has always hindered me from going out and living my life to the fullest. I've always seen myself as broken, and to be honest, I still do.

But as the professor starts lecturing, I fight the urge to run and instead listen to his voice. He's younger than most of the teachers here, and he seems to be less serious as he offers us all a smile.

Domenico Toscano is handsome. Even though he's not as old as some of the other professors, I'm pretty sure he's nearly thirty. He teaches with ease, his gaze tracking each of us as he speaks, and I can't help but listen intently. He's charming, and there's a magnetism about him that seems to have all the female students hanging on his every word.

But, as handsome as he is, he doesn't compare to the three men who are at home, waiting for me. I thought it was bad enough having to get married to someone I didn't know, someone who's from a family that hates my father, but now I've discovered that three men will own me. I hate thinking of it that way, but it's true. The men in this world are possessive when it comes to their property.

As Professor Toscano speaks, I can't help but notice he's looking in only one direction. The student who's seated right in front is staring at him, and he's talking directly to her. The connection is clear— they're attracted to one another. And when he makes a move to hand out the assignments, he lingers at her table just a bit longer than at anyone else's.

There's something strange about the interaction, and a niggling in my gut has me wondering about the professor himself. As the class continues, I can't help allowing my mind to wander back to my new home. I didn't think I would ever call the Venier mansion home, but here we are.

Perhaps I'm still in shock. My shower fantasy has taken on a surreal turn. I never believed something like that could actually happen to me. I don't judge the three Princes. I can't think negatively about their feelings towards each other. If I'm being honest, I find it rather sexy, but thoughts of what the future holds keep taking over my mind, and I know I need to talk to them about our complicated dynamic.

As the day passes, I'm still not sure what to do, and that's bothering me.

Can I survive being with three men?

My mind continues to dwell on the situation I've found myself in, so when a hand grabs hold of my arm and spins me around, it takes me a moment to focus. When I do, I realise I'm now face-to-face with the guy Kai threatened for approaching me at the restaurant. His gaze drags over me, slowly, deliberately, and it causes a shiver of revulsion to course through me.

"What are you doing?" I bite out as I attempt to tug away from his hold, but he's got a grip on me that makes me wince.

His fingers dig into my flesh as he pulls me up against him. No one around us bothers helping, they don't seem concerned that this arsehole has a fierce hold on me.

"Your little boyfriend isn't here to protect you now, princess," he sneers down at me.

The bastard thinks I need a bodyguard to keep me safe. But when I told Judah I can take care of myself, I meant it. I'm not a helpless child.

I recall my classes of self-defence. When I turned

thirteen, I was sent to learn how to protect myself from any attack. Papa always made sure I knew how to fight off anyone who wanted to hurt me. He knew I would be in danger when people learnt my identity. He said, should anything happen to me, I would have the skills to defend myself. He knew, deep down, I might need it one day because of who I am.

I spin around, taking the arm of this bastard with me. Then pulling him closer, so his front is slammed against my back, I step backwards with one of my heeled boots and make contact with his trainer. Before I tug his forearm over my shoulder and jerk his hand down. The groan from behind me makes me smile, and I apply more pressure to his arm. It doesn't break, but I almost wish it did.

When I finally release him, I turn around and pin him with a glare.

"Don't ever think I need a man to stand up for me or to protect me." My words cause his eyes to widen in shock. "I may be a princess, but I'm not weak." I turn and leave him nursing his arm.

"That was amazing," a female voice catches my attention and I turn to see one of the girls from my history class. "I'm Emilia," she tells me with a small smile, holding out her hand.

I take it, and we shake as I introduce myself.

"Brielle," I tell her. "He's just an arsehole who

thinks he can scare women because he's taller, stronger, and a man."

"As do most of the men on this island. That's why they're here, to learn how to exert their dominance," she tells me as we make our way to the parking lot. "You're new here?"

"Yes, I arrived a couple of weeks ago," I tell her with a nod. I'm living at—"

"The Venier manor," she finishes. "I know. Everyone's heard about the new girl on the island."

I can't help but groan at that piece of information, even though I know it's true. The guys told me I'd be the talk of the campus.

"I honestly don't want to bring any attention to myself. I just want to study."

"Unfortunately, now that you're with Judah Venier, there's no hiding, especially on this island," she tells me with a shrug of her shoulders.

We stop at a sleek, black Porsche that has a matte finish, shiny silver rims, and the windows tinted so dark I can't see inside.

"I'm not really with him," I say, but she laughs.

I know it sounds like a lie because I am his fiancée. Soon, I'll be saying my vows and agreeing to be his wife. But we haven't ever been intimate, and he hasn't kissed me yet. So, it doesn't feel like I'm truly *with* him.

"Oh, trust me, you are." Emilia laughs as she opens the door. "Need a ride home?"

"She already has one."

I didn't expect to find Judah standing behind me, but his voice is clear, and when I do glance over my shoulder, I'm knocked breathless. He's not in his usual attire. He's in a deep green polo shirt with a pair of black jeans.

"Right," Emilia says. "I'll see you tomorrow, Brielle."

Emilia doesn't wait for me to respond. Instead, she slips into the driver's seat, starts the engine, and reverses out of the parking bay before speeding away, causing the tyres to squeal against the tar.

I spin around to glare at Judah.

"I could have gone home with her, you didn't need to play the knight in shining armour."

Judah leans in close, and to the outside observer, it may look like he's being sweet, as if he's going to kiss my cheek, but I know better. His voice is a low whisper.

"I got a call you had an issue, I'm here to sort it out." He straightens, and smirks down at me as he regards me with those hazel eyes.

"The *issue*," I say, holding up my fingers as if adding quotation marks to the word, "has been dealt with. Like I told you, I'm capable of taking care of myself."

"Fair enough," he appeases, surprising me for a moment. "But I'm still here to drive you home. Kai is waiting for you."

"Why?"

He doesn't respond, but instead, he opens the passenger door of his Maserati, and I slip obediently inside because I know he won't answer me until I'm safely tucked away in his car.

Once inside, he starts the engine, and soon, we're leaving the university campus and heading back to the other side of the island. It won't take us long to get home, but while we're travelling together, I want nothing more than for Judah to talk to me.

As we drive along the coastal road, I glance over at him. I'm still surprised at just how beautiful he is. If he wasn't such a bastard, I'd more than likely fall for him without question.

"Why is Kai waiting for me?"

"He's going to start training you," Judah says without looking at me. His focus is on the road ahead of us, but I know if I was in any danger, or if I was to suddenly push open my car door just to test him, his reflexes would be as sharp as his jaw. "We're all going to train you, in our own way."

"Train me? I don't need—"

"This isn't about what you need, Brielle." The frustration in Judah's tone matches my own.

Suddenly, he pulls off the road. He kills the engine, twists in his seat, and orders, "Get out."

My mouth pops open, but my own stubbornness forces me to ignore him, and I sit back in my seat and stare out the windscreen. I don't respond, I just watch the waves crashing towards the island. I can't see the rocks from here, but I know they're there, and anyone who gets too close to the edge could easily fall and end up dead.

Before I realise what's happening, Judah is out of the vehicle and heading round to my side. Soon enough, my door opens, and I'm dragged from my seat. He pulls me along behind him until we're standing on what feels like the edge of the world. All I can see for miles is water. The deep, dark blue Mediterranean Sea stretches out to the horizon. The sun is slowly lowering, gifting the sky a strange, fiery hue.

Judah spins me around, his front to my back, and even though it's not the first time I've been this close to him, he still steals my breath. His warmth is like a cocoon as he pulls me against his body. I'm not sure what he's doing, what he's planning to do, but I can see the water below us and the rocks now, too—the dark brown, jagged edges so clear as the white water slams against them.

"What are you doing?" I ask in a soft tone, realising I'm truly frightened. Of the three men I'm living with, Judah scares me the most. "Judah," I whisper his name when he takes a step closer to the edge, forcing me to follow suit.

His grip on me tightens as he leans forward, his chest pushing against my back, until I'm bent over the cliff edge, and I gasp as the rocks loom closer. It would be so easy for him to let go, and I'd fall to my death.

"Do you see how simple it is?" Judah whispers in my ear.

The warmth of his breath soothes my trembling, but the fear is still there. Judah has this dangerous aura about him—he wears it like a cologne. And I know he'll kill me if he ever finds out I've been keeping things from him.

"Judah, let's go home," I tell him, and suddenly, he spins me round so my front is pressed up against his.

My breathing speeds up, and I know he can feel every movement. I wonder if he can detect my heartbeat thrumming in my chest.

"If I ever find out that you're here as a spy, this is where your life will end," he threatens, holding me over the edge of the cliff.

The water crashing below is so loud it booms in my ears, and along with my erratic heartbeat, the noise is deafening. A chill skitters down my spine as I look up into those eyes that hold anger and something else I never expected to see—fear.

"I'm not," I tell him. It's the only truth I can offer him for now.

I only came to Black Hollow because Papa forced my hand. I didn't expect him to force me to marry a stranger. And I don't know if I can ever forgive my father for it.

"Don't you forget this, Brielle," Judah warns me as he leans in closer. "Those men at home love me, and I them. And if you threaten that happiness, I won't think twice about ending your life."

His lips feather across mine. The warmth of his breath and the heat of his body, causing every nerve in my body to spark with desire.

Suddenly, I'm pulled back from the cliff's edge and Judah steps away from me, leaving me to shiver from the cold breeze that hits us both. His hair is a mess as it falls across his forehead, the dark locks hiding one of his eyes.

"Let's go," he tells me and heads back to the car.

I follow along and slip into the passenger seat before pulling the door closed. He doesn't speak to me. He doesn't even look at me. The engine purrs to life, and soon, we're back on the road and heading home.

We're not far from the house when I finally say softly, "The way you hate me confuses me."

I sit back and focus on the road ahead instead of on Judah. I'm afraid to look at him because that moment on the edge of the cliff made my feelings for him a lot clearer.

Judah pulls up to the house, the drive home now thankfully behind us as he circles the fountain that sits just outside the front entrance. When he kills the engine, he twists in his seat and looks at me.

"I've done many evil things in my life," he admits. "I've killed people who've been disloyal, I've tortured people who've betrayed my family, and I will do so again. But I'll make something very clear to you right now, I didn't hate them," he tells me as he grips my chin and forces me to look at him. "And I don't hate you, Brielle," he confesses. "I just don't trust you."

"I'm not my father," I bite out as frustration takes over. "You, Valen, and Kai trusted me with a secret. You've told me something I could easily go and blab about, but I haven't, and I won't. I'm not here to spy on you. My father forced me to come here, to marry you. I didn't have a choice."

"The same way we don't have a choice," Judah says, and I realise, no matter how angry I am at him, he's only doing what he's been trained to do all his life—protect his family.

I was lucky enough not to grow up in this world,

177

I didn't get pushed into killing people from a young age. He did. So did Valen and Kai.

"I am sorry," I whisper as he looks away and stares out the windscreen.

Judah releases his hold on me, and I immediately miss his touch. When we first met, I'd hoped we could get to a place where we could be civil with one another, but I never expected to develop feelings for him. As much as we may argue, I realise I really do like Judah Venier.

"I don't need you to apologise," he tells me, and just like that, the guy who was showing emotion is gone, and the cold, calculating mafia Underboss is back. "We need to go. There's a party in town tonight, and you need to work out with Kai before we go."

He pushes open his door and leaves me in the car. Even when I don't follow behind, he doesn't look back, and I'm once again confused as to what I'm going to do about him. I'm not sure how to get through to him. The gentle affection I show Valen is not going to work on Judah.

Sighing, I make my way to the front entrance of the mansion, and pushing open the door, I head inside. There's no point in looking for Judah, so instead, I make my way to my bedroom to change into some sweatpants and a T-shirt.

My mind is still on Judah when I finally walk into

the gym and find Malachi doing weight training with Valen.

"There she is," Valen says as he pushes to his feet and rushes towards me.

The man is like my own personal cheerleader. Out of the three of them, he's made me feel the most at ease. But I know, even though Valen doesn't look as dangerous as the other two, there's an underlying menace to him.

I'm about to reply when my phone buzzes, and I pull it from my pocket. Judah's name is brightly lit on the screen. It's a message from him.

When I open it, warmth courses through me, causing my cheeks to heat. It's a photo of him on his bed, one leg crooked at the knee, and his arm outstretched with the phone in one hand. He's not wearing anything but a pair of dark jeans. The mirror at the end of his bed shows me the reflection of the beautiful, yet dangerous man, half hidden in the shadows.

The text attached to the photo reads, *Don't forget how your body feels against mine.*

I don't reply. Instead, I hide my phone back in my pocket and greet Valen with a hug.

"Who was that?" Valen questions.

"Judah. Reminding me I'm going to some party tonight," I lie quickly, hoping to forget about the photo, but deep down, as I move to the mat where Kai is waiting, I can't force it out of my mind.

"Are you ready?" Kai asks as he smiles at me.

"I am. I've done some self-defence before, so this shouldn't be too bad."

"Let's go, princess."

Kai starts by grabbing my arm and tugging me against his rock-hard body. There are dips and peaks of muscle I can't help but feel when he moves. I'm confident I can handle his next move. But, I don't expect Valen to suddenly come from behind and grab me. Both of them twist me in their grasp. I'm able to pull away from one, but the other still has hold of me. This is definitely not going to be easy.

I'm out of breath within ten minutes, and I'm ready to fall to the ground and beg for mercy. Kai notices, and he and Valen both step back, allowing me time to catch my breath. As I bend over with my hands on my thighs, Kai watches me with his head tipped to the side.

With both of them attacking, I found it difficult to defend myself. I was able to shake one off, but I was struggling with two. My muscles are aching, and deep down, I'm disappointed in myself. I know I am better than this.

Kai hands me a towel. "Not bad for a girl," he tells me as he chuckles.

"Let's go again. I can prove to you I'm able to

look after myself," I say, hoping the Princes will stop treating me as if I'm defenceless. I'm not. I'm stronger than they all think.

Kai smiles, before he smirks and says, "You can hold your own, but if we had weapons, you wouldn't stand a chance, sweetheart."

"Then teach me how to use them," I beg.

When I was younger, I hated anything to do with weapons. But now my father is no longer here to protect me, I have to look after myself. I'm going to become a target when I marry Judah, so I'll have to know how to make a kill. I'm not going to rely on these men. I don't want to.

"I'll talk to Jude," Kai tells me. "But I don't see it being a problem. We'll start next week."

DRIVE YOU INSANE

JUDAH

She's nervous around me. I wanted so badly to play a game with her, to see how she'd react. The edge of the cliff is dangerous, but I enjoy the rush of not knowing if fate will step in and steal me away. Holding her body so close was intoxicating. I didn't expect her to keep as calm as she did. But feeling her chest rising and falling against mine had my dick rock fucking hard. And there's no doubt she felt it. I'm convinced she's just as attracted to me as I am to her.

When I took her to the cliff edge, I wanted to make her realise she could so easily be killed. I still have my doubts about her, but I know she's been forced to come here because of the fucking contract. Perhaps that's why I don't trust her, because she didn't choose us—she didn't choose me. Brielle was thrown into the lion's den, and now she's having to fight to stay alive.

As we pull up to the street party, that's already in full swing, I don't bother looking at her. I'm focused on the crowds that have gathered. The street races will start soon, and I'm looking forward to seeing who will rise up the ranks. At the moment, I hold the record and Valen's in third place. Kai doesn't race, but he does ensure our vehicles are looked after and faster than the usual run-of-the-mill sports cars.

When Valen helps Brielle from the car, I have to fight the urge to tell her to cover the fuck up. The moment she came down the stairs earlier, it took all my willpower not to show her how she affected me. I don't like it, and I don't fucking need this distraction. I told her to dress up, but I didn't mean for her to show off so much skin. She may as well be naked.

"This is so cool," she says as she smiles up at Val, and my stomach twists.

She considers him a friend, or perhaps something even closer. She drives me insane, yet I'm intrigued by her. The shiny black leggings she's wearing have a slit down the outside of each leg, from her hip to her ankle. The edges of the material are laced together, but the thin string barely keeps them in place. Her long legs look delicious, and I can't deny I'm thinking about the day they're wrapped around my waist.

Her top is a red, loose-fitting, strap tank that billows in the breeze, and I can tell she's not wearing a bra. Granted, her tits aren't exposed, but still, the thought of them being uncovered, bared to me, has been playing in my mind since I got in the car.

"Do you want a drink?" Val asks her, and as he takes her hand, darkness clouds my vision because he has to realise we need to keep our wits about us. We can't risk getting her drunk, especially when these arseholes around us are gawking at our girl.

"She's not drinking," I bite out in annoyance, and pin Val with a glare. "Focus."

There are too many students around tonight, and she's already had an altercation with one of them. There's no need to have her defences lowered by alcohol.

"I'd like a drink," Brielle announces, looking at me, but addressing Valen. "Thank you." She turns to my best friend, and smiles.

I reach out, grab her arm, and drag her to my car. Her back hits the driver's door, and she glares up at me. I don't miss the hint of fear, but I also notice the desire that swirls in her eyes. Fuck.

"When I say no," I tell her, keeping my voice low. It looks like I'm being a possessive boyfriend to everyone else around us, but I know she can see the crazed dominance that's coiling deep within me. "It's no. And I expect you to listen to me, obey me, and trust me."

"How do I trust you when you don't trust me," she throws back, and I can't argue with her. She's right. I still can't bring myself to trust her, because I still don't know her well enough.

I lean in further, my mouth at her cheek, and her sweet scented perfume fills my nostrils.

"Trust, my darling, is earned," I whisper in her ear, causing her to shiver against me.

I should have brought her a jacket, but I didn't think about it. When I saw what she was wearing, the only thing on my mind was bending her over and ripping those fucking leggings from her body.

"So is respect," she murmurs as she rises up on her tiptoes, and her words feather along my ear, down my neck, and cause my dick to throb with need.

I move back slightly and take in her face. Her mouth is pure perfection, and I can clearly envision my cock sliding between those sensuous lips. I hate her, but I also want to fuck her within an inch of her life.

Jesus.

What the fuck is wrong with me?

I reach up and cup her cheek, and for a second, she leans into my touch. Running my thumb along her lower lip, I smile when she opens for me and I dip into that luscious warmth. Her tongue dances across the tip of my thumb, cause my cock to harden ever so slightly.

"You have no idea how much I want you on your knees right now," I tell her.

It's one of the first emotionally charged things I've said to her. Whenever we speak, it always involves a spew of anger or hatred. But right now, it's pure lust.

Her teeth bite down on my thumb, hard, and I can't stop the smile on my face. She's a fighter. I like that, a lot.

"If you ever try that with my dick down your throat," I inform her coolly. "I will make you pay in ways that will remind you of what you did wrong. Make no mistake, I can hurt you, sweetheart." With that, I pull away, causing her mouth to pop open and her pretty eyes to widen. "Go to Valen," I tell her.

The dismissive nature of my command has her brows furrowing together, and I half expect her to refuse, but she doesn't. Instead, she leaves me standing at the car, my hand on the roof, and my mind in a fucking mess.

The races are about to start with two Ferraris at the ready. I ignore Valen's questioning stare as I make my way to the front of the crowd. I should be focused on the race as the cars speed off, but I'm watching Brielle. Valen has his arm around her shoulders.

There's nothing sexually intimate about it, but I can't help my hands from fisting at my sides.

I'm not jealous.

I'm not angry.

I just want her to look at me the way she does them.

I don't know what these fucking emotions running through me are, and I don't like them. Spinning on my heel, I head down the road to a quiet section that leads off to the coastal edge of the island. The races will continue late into the night, the winner of each round taking on a new opponent. I intended to take part, but I'm not in the right mindset.

I watch the waves crashing against the rocks. It's dark below, black as night, with only the white spray visible as the water attacks the land. I tried to scare her at the cliff edge. I mostly succeeded, but I'm now convinced this girl isn't going to run and hide.

She challenges me. And she makes me want more.

"Are you okay?" Her voice is like a Siren's song from behind me. I don't turn to look at her, I keep my eyes on the blackness below. "I noticed you walk off, and wanted to say that—"

"You don't have to look after me as if I'm a child," I tell her as anger takes over. From when I was young, my father taught me that showing affection will get you killed. And when I realised my feelings for Kai and Valen had changed, I knew, deep down, Dad was right. My affection for them could so easily get us all killed.

"You spend your life so angry at the world, Judah," Brielle tells me. "Why not stop for a moment and allow something good to come into your heart."

I spin around, causing her eyes to widen in surprise.

"I'm angry because that's what I've learnt to be. I run the university, this island, and my father's organisation. Soon, I'll be the Boss. I can't risk allowing my enemies in."

Her voice is a low whisper of pain when she asks, "Am I your enemy?"

Her question stops me short. I wasn't expecting it. I'm not sure how to answer her, because I don't see her as an enemy. She's just someone I can't have around me. And I don't want to delve into that mind fuck of a reason.

"I know you don't want me here," she says. "But I'm staying, and I just need to know you'll come to accept me at some point. I can't live with a man, a husband, who doesn't even consider me worth talking to."

Why is she doing this to me? How the fuck is she doing this to me?

"There's no rhyme or reason to emotions, princess," I tell her. "Things can change within a blink of an eye. So, no matter what is going on between us at the moment, it doesn't mean that weeks, or perhaps months, from now it will be the same."

Frustration has twisted its roots deep within me, and I've no way of dealing with her, other than to show anger. Perhaps it's because I'm raging at my father for bringing her into my life. Or maybe it's because, deep down, I want to want her.

I can't allow myself to get distracted by a pretty face, though. She may be my wife soon, but that doesn't mean anything, not in this world. I've seen men kill their wives when the organisation demanded it. But then again, I'm not like them. I'm not even my father, despite the years I struggled to become like him.

For so long, I only had Val and Kai to give me strength. They burrowed themselves into my heart, and once they were in, there was no way of getting them out. My soul had found its matches, so I had no choice. I thought all I needed was them, but now I have to include Brielle, and I'm not sure how to do it.

"I don't know what else to think, Judah," she tells me, dragging me out of my thoughts and into the present moment. "You've made sure I've been on the outside of whatever you think this is," she says as she waves a hand between us. "But we're both in the same boat. We've both had our choices taken away from us, and you can't blame me for that, no matter how much you'd like to."

"Don't try to understand me," I throw back as I once again attempt to fight whatever this is between us. But I know there's no use in even trying, because she's been crawling under my skin, under my defences, since I first saw her.

"I do understand you more than you know," she retorts. "We're in this together, and if you can't fucking respect that, then send me back. Let me go."

I look at her. I really and truly look at her and see the darkness that swirls in her eyes. I've always fought the desire to meet those orbs, and now I know why. It's because I didn't want to see who she truly is. She's not the spoiled princess I thought she was. There's much more to her than the family name she holds.

"Go back to the party," I tell her, dismissing her before I'm tempted to steal a kiss.

I can't do it because I won't be able to stop myself. I need to talk to the guys. I need to sit down and plan what we're going to do about her. She's not someone who we chose. She's been thrust upon us, and we need to decide how to handle her. She has to become part of our dynamic, and we all have to be in agreement as to how that will work.

Brielle smiles as she lowers her gaze and looks down at the ground by our feet. The grassy cliff edge is dark, even though I know it's a lush green in the daylight.

"I thought for a while you were an angry, cold-hearted arsehole," Brielle says, causing me to lift my gaze to hers. "But you're not."

"Oh, trust me, princess," I inform her as I take a step towards her. "I am angry, and I'll always be cold-hearted, there's no doubt about that, and you should never second guess it."

"Noted," Brielle responds, but the smile on her face tells me there's more she'd like to add. "I'll go back to the party, but this conversation isn't over," she says as she turns and walks away.

As the words leave her lips, I want nothing more than to bend her over, right here and now, and spank her pert little arse. But I refrain, for now. She may think she's in charge, but that's far from the truth.

Once I'm alone with my thoughts, I consider what this all means. It's a breakthrough. I didn't expect her to take a chance and open up to me about her thoughts.

"Are you two finally being civil?" Kai saunters up behind me with a smirk on his face.

"I don't know," I tell him honestly.

Even though I want nothing more than for all this suspicion to be over, for the trust to grow, I still don't know if it's possible. It may never be. But then again, perhaps that's just me focusing on the wrong things.

Both Kai and Val have accepted her. And to be fair, she hasn't told anyone about the secret we confessed to her, which she could have done.

"The thing is, unless you let her in, we'll never learn the truth about her and what she believes," Kai tells me as he kicks at the ground. "She's a good fighter. She's worth having on our side."

I know they've trained with her. I sent her that photo to distract her because I thought she'd still be reeling from our little chat on the cliff edge. But it seems she wasn't as perturbed as I thought she'd be.

I'll have to rectify that.

I'm done with this party. My focus isn't on anything it should be, and it doesn't sit well with me.

"I"m going home," I announce to Kai, surprising him.

The others can get home without me, so there's no need for me to stick around.

"What about—?"

"You can watch her. I'm just not in the mood for this bullshit tonight," I tell him before I turn and head back into the crowds to where my car is parked.

I can feel Kai's presence behind me, and I wonder just what he's thinking. He's never seen me this bothered by a woman before, and neither has Valen.

This is new territory for all of us.

But then again, I never had a fiancée before, which makes matters worse.

"I'm leaving," I tell Valen who's standing beside Brielle.

"Can I come with you?" she asks, her eyes lit up by the headlights of the cars as they pull in close to where we're standing.

I can't have her in the house alone with me, but I also can't refuse her. After our earlier talk, I owe her the civility of being a gentleman.

"Sure." I nod and turn away before I get an earful from Kai.

He knows this is the last thing I wanted, or needed, but there's nothing I can do to stop it.

In the car, I don't speak to her, I don't even bother looking her way. I can't. Confusion settles in my gut like a lead weight, and I'm not sure how the fuck to handle this. I'm going to have to sit down with the guys tomorrow. I can't go on like this, hiding from her while in my own home, on my own fucking island. Enough is enough.

When I finally pull into the grounds of the mansion, she says, "Thank you, Judah."

My name on her lips is the sweetest thing I've ever fucking heard, and I want to steal the words from her mouth.

I stop the car at the entrance to the house and hand her a set of keys.

"Go inside," I tell her.

I wait for her to argue, but she doesn't, and I'm

shocked by this. Her fire has been constant, but right now, she's being obedient, and I wonder what brought on the change.

It can't be our talk.

It can't be feelings.

There can be no emotions between us, not yet, and not right now.

No.

I watch her go inside, and I lean my head back against the seat. I don't know what to do with her, but I'm equally convinced she's not sure how to handle me either.

BLOOD ON MY HANDS

BRIELLE

Since the night of the party, I've been mainly focused on my studies and training with Kai.

He got permission from Judah to show me how to use a knife. It's small and sleek, making it easy to hide and carry around with me. The plan is to have it on me at all times, which means I'll be armed if anything was to happen.

I haven't been able to find any time to be alone with Judah so we can talk again. He's been avoiding me, and it hurts, deep down, but I understand why. He didn't expect me to take the first step towards making our relationship amicable. If I'm being honest, I didn't think I would do it either.

When I get back to the house from university, it's almost dark out and I know they're going to lose their minds. I was meant to meet with Kai, but I got sidetracked in the library, and now I'm running late for everything.

I push open the door, and the moment I step inside, I'm practically assaulted by testosterone emanating from not one but three alpha males as they glare at me.

"Sorry I'm late." It's all I can offer, and it's a lot more than they're owed.

I'm not a child, and they don't have to worry about me, especially since I'm now armed and ready for anything. But the look on Judah's face tells me my apology's not going to work.

I should just turn around and walk back out, but instead, I shut the door behind me and set my bag down near the stairs. They don't speak, they just stare.

"I was in the library. I needed to finish my assignment and lost track of time, but now I'm here. I'm safe and sound." I've no idea why I'm still talking, it's not like it's going to make any difference to them.

"Come," Judah finally says as he takes my arm and tugs me down the long hallway, passing by his office, until we get to an ominous, wooden door.

I watch as he unlocks it and it swings open, and then we're moving forward once more. Only now, we're taking steps down into the darkness. He moves slowly, giving me time to catch up. The other two men are following close behind, and I can feel the anger radiating from all of them.

When we reach the bottom, a switch is flicked, and we're bathed in a soft yellow glow. There's a strange, damp smell coming from all around us, and I shiver when an icy chill travels up my spine.

"What is this?" I ask as we come to a stop at the end of a gloomy hallway that's lined with doors.

I can't see anything beyond the closed, metal doors, so I can only imagine what goes on down here.

"This is where people who don't obey us spend some time," Judah tells me as he pulls one of the heavy steel doors open.

It screeches as it trails across the floor. Inside, the cell is tiny, but it's enough to house a bed and a bucket that I can only assume is for bodily functions.

When I look at Judah, I realise what he's trying to tell me without coming right out and saying it. My stomach drops, and my heart leaps into my throat as fear takes over. I thought we were past the hate and anger, but clearly, we're not.

"You're not putting me in there," I bite out, but I'm quickly shoved forward, sent sprawling into the room and locked inside. A small window opens in the secured door, and all I can see are the hazel eyes of my fiancé, looking through the gap. "You fucking bastard!"

"If you can't learn to obey our rules, then you'll have to spend some time in here," he tells me, his voice has an icy chill to it.

"Come on, man, let's leave her," Valen says.

There's tension amongst them. Clearly, all three of them were worried when I was late, but it isn't as if they didn't know where I was.

"Do you understand that if something happens to you, it's on all of us?" Judah speaks once more, his gaze trained back on me.

"You're a fucking arsehole," I bite out. "I was in the library." He slams the small window shut, and everything goes silent. "Don't you dare leave me in here!"

I'm convinced that screaming isn't going to work. These places are built to muffle the sound of torture, so my voice won't do much against the thick concrete walls that surround me.

I don't know what to do. Anger overwhelms me. Just when I think I'm taking a step forward, making ground with Judah, he pushes me two steps in the other direction, and I'm once more on the back foot.

Frustration and fear courses through me as I sit down on the mattress that creaks beneath me. I can't lie down, because I'm too fearful of whoever was in this cell before me. So, I sit and wait. Surely, Kai and Valen will talk him out of this insanity.

Judah can't keep me in here forever. That's what I

tell myself, over and over again, as time passes. but the longer I sit here, the lonelier and more scared I feel.

Sighing, I stand and pace back and forth. The tears I kept at bay, all this time, finally spring free and trickle down my cheeks.

I'm not sure how long I've been imprisoned, when suddenly, the door lurches open and standing on the other side is Valen.

"Come," he calls, and I rush towards him.

I slam into Valen's body, and his arms wrap around me. He doesn't say anything. For a long while, he merely stands there, holding me as if I'm a wounded bird. His hand circles my back as I sob, and I realise just how afraid I was. As much as I like him, Judah still fucking scares me. And I don't think he'll ever *not* scare me.

"It's…" I choke out. "It's not right. I didn't do anything wrong."

"I know," he says softly as he steps back. "Judah's angry because we found a few students doing background checks on you. One of them is in the room down the hall." Valen gestures with his head towards the darker part of the dungeon we're standing in.

"But I don't understand," I say. "Why would he lock me in here. I don't—"

Then, Valen chuckles, which catches me off guard.

"We've all had our time in these cells. It's part of your initiation—the start of you becoming one of us."

"What?"

"Step one, spend some time in that shithole." Valen's voice lowers as he speaks. "Step two, Judah's going to want to see what you're made of, so whatever he demands, just obey him. His orders are law here."

"I don't like playing games," I tell Valen. "If he's bringing me into the family, into the organisation, he can do it without messing with my head."

I tug away from him in anger. I don't want to be pushed around by any of them. I won't be the pawn in their twisted game.

"Are you ready to get some blood on your hands, princess?" Judah's voice stops me short. I want nothing more than to slap him, but it will probably land me back in the cell, so all I do is offer him a nod.

I don't want to talk to him. Or be near him. But for now, I'll play along with this fucked up game he's decided is an initiation into this family unit.

I'm led by Judah down the hall and into the darkest depths of the dungeon. He takes me to a room that's much larger than the cell I was in, and there, sitting bound to a chair, is the guy who tried to attack me at university last week.

"What is going on?" I ask, my gaze flicking to Judah.

Judah stops in front of the man. "This is Marco DiMario," he announces.

The man looking back at me causes me to shiver. It could all be over now.

"What is he doing here?" I whisper.

"Your little boyfriends think I'm some kind of spy," Marco spits in anger as he pins me with a glare. It's the same look he gave me that day on campus. "Did you go squealing to them, about me wanting to talk to you? I don't appreciate being treated like a criminal when I'm here to learn, just like everyone else."

"Then explain why we found photos of Brielle Saviatti, from when she was living in the UK, and a copy of her medical file in your possession?"

Shock slams right into my chest when I cast a glance at Judah. If this bastard has my medical file, that means Judah's seen it. That means they've all seen it. They know what happened.

My head spins with the possibilities of them knowing the most intimate details of my life. I didn't expect my secret to come out like this, but now that it so clearly has, I'm not sure how to react.

"I haven't told anyone her secrets, yet," Marco says as he sneers at me, making my body quake with the thought of everyone on this island knowing I'm broken.

"And you won't be telling anyone," Valen says

before he steps up to the side of the chair. His eyes are on me.

Now I know why they were so angry, it wasn't that I was out late, it wasn't because I didn't call them to ask for a ride home, it's because they know.

"It's time for you to earn your place, princess," Judah tells me as he hands me a blade far larger than the ones I've been training with.

He wants me to hurt Marco. No, not just hurt him. Judah wants me to torture, possibly kill, the man in front of me.

I snap my gaze to Judah's, and I open my mouth to speak, but I can't find the words I need. My throat closes as panic takes over. I've never hurt someone for the sake of it, but when Judah looks at me, I realise this is more about keeping secrets than it is about anything else.

"There's no choice in this life," he tells me, as if he can read my mind.

I have no doubt he probably can read my mind. That's one thing about Judah Venier, he's perceptive. Kai steps up behind me, his hands landing on my hips as he holds me steady. I'm swaying, dizziness hitting me full force now, and I wish I could run away. I don't want to do this, but when I look back at Marco, I know he's not someone who can be trusted to keep a secret.

I can't risk it. There's too much at stake to allow

Marco to live. I know it, the Princes know it, and Marco does as well. He looks at me as if he knows I'm weak, but the smirk on his face only adds fuel to the fire that's slowly burning inside me.

"If you don't do it—" Judah warns, but he doesn't complete his sentence.

If I don't, they'll have no choice. I step forward, my hand gripping the handle of the knife so tightly I'm pretty sure my knuckles are white. Valen grips Marco's hair, and pulling his head back, he exposes the condemned man's fragile neck. The moment I succumb to this, I'll have blood on my hands, which is exactly what they want. I know their secret, and now they'll own mine.

"Are you going to fall into the darkness, princess?" Judah speaks, but it sounds so far away. As if I'm in a tunnel, and they're watching me from the outside. I feel like I'm in a nightmare, and there's no way I can turn back.

"Do it," Marco goads me. "I don't think a little girl who's as broken as you can ever become their queen," he throws the insult out, and my mind goes blank.

I don't think about it as my hand moves of its own accord, and I feel the sharp steel slice through the soft flesh of Marco's neck. The sound is surreal, like nothing I've heard before. I've never been around death, yet here I am meting it out.

Blood spurts from the wound. The way Marco's head droops, makes my stomach turn. I drop the knife before racing to the nearest wall, and bending over, I puke up my lunch. As I continue to retch, the acidic burn causes tears to sting my eyes. I never considered myself capable of violence, but I'm in their world now.

There's no going back.

I feel hands on my hips, holding me steady. It has to be Val. I can't stop coughing. The metallic scent of blood fills my nostrils, and I can't escape it. I'll never be free of it now. I'm stained, just like every other student on this island.

Just like my father.

When I finally straighten, I turn to find Kai holding out a bottle of water towards me. Val is still gripping my hips in his strong hands while Judah watches from the other side of the room, his eyes giving nothing away.

Disappointment flows through me. I'm not sure I can explain it, but perhaps I want Judah to show me an expression of pride now I've taken this irrevocable step into their world. It's stupid to want that, and I don't know why I do. I've obeyed him. Surely, I should get a reward.

"Drink," Kai says, gesturing to the bottle, and I accept it with a small smile and a shaky hand.

I don't want them to know what I'm thinking, so I

try to calm my breathing before taking a long sip. The refreshing liquid soothes the burn in my throat, and I close my eyes, not wanting to see my blood-stained hands.

"Take her to her room. I'll be up in a minute," Judah commands in a low baritone that sends my heart into a wildly thrumming beat.

I'm led in silence back through the house to my bedroom that's become a safe haven for me. I want to wash my hands, but I don't dare move. I stand in the middle of the room with Kai on one side of me and Valen the other. I'm cocooned in warmth from both sides.

This wasn't supposed to happen like this. I wanted to sit them down and tell them everything when I was sure I could trust them. Even though they've given me no reason to doubt them, I never wanted my health to become an issue.

SUFFOCATE ME

BRIELLE

STANDING BETWEEN BOTH MEN MAKES ME SHIVER WITH the anticipation of what they're going to do to me. I'm still caked in blood, but they either don't notice, or they aren't perturbed. I'm going with the latter. They're probably used to being drenched in the blood of their enemies, so this is nothing new.

"It had to be done," Kai tells me, being the first to speak and capture my attention.

"I... I know, it's just..." I shake my head when I think about killing someone.

When I was younger, I recall my father telling me there'll be times I'll have to do things I don't like. That I'll have to do some things that may go against all I believe in. I know my father did it for years before he escaped.

"Let's get you cleaned up," Valen says, taking over from Kai and leading me into the bathroom.

This is where I'm finally forced to look at my reflection in the mirror above the basin while Val stands silently beside me. I have blood splattered all over me in fine little dots of red. The crimson on my hands, though, that's the most sickening. I know I'm about to wash them, but they'll always be stained with the memory.

"It goes away," Kai says as he leans against the door frame.

"What does?" I throw back. "The guilt? The shame? Or the sickening realisation that I'm a murderer?"

I glare at him and wait for him to say I'm wrong, but he doesn't. He knows there isn't anything he can tell me that could alter how I feel about this. I knew my life would change when I walked into this house...no, before I even got on the plane.

Judah appears at the door, just behind Kai, and he pins me with a stare. I take in the crisp white, button-up shirt he's wearing, which is now stained in crimson.

"When you learn this life is fragile, nothing matters anymore. The moment you detach yourself from the action of taking revenge or allowing mercy, only then will you realise you have all the control. You need to know in our world, there are no innocent people, there are only those who deserve what's coming to them. That's how you survive."

"And if I can't learn all that, or come to terms with it?" I whisper, my throat aching from my earlier breakdown. The water helped, but there's still a sting when I try to speak.

"Then you may not get through this," Judah warns.

For a long moment, we stand in the bathroom, all four of us in the same space, and with three tall, alpha males watching me, I suddenly feel as if I'm a deer caught in headlights. I'm prey in the lion's den.

"I've always believed that mercy should be bestowed on everyone," I tell him as I tip my chin up in a show of defiance, but as much as I want to show strength, I can't. I feel weak, more so than I have in a long time. "I just don't know how to think like you."

"You'll have to make a decision," Judah says as he pushes past everyone and turns on the shower.

He doesn't seem at all bothered by slowly undressing in front of me. His shirt falls to the floor in a silent whisper as the water sprays down onto the tiles. The steam clouds the room as we stand there, silently watching Judah.

"If you want a shower, you're more than welcome to join us, Brielle," he offers with a smirk as he regards me.

Valen pulls me into his arms, not at all bothered that I'm getting him covered in blood. He tugs me against him, and leaning in, he says, "Would you like to take a journey with us?"

In a split second, I forget about the blood, the knife, and the dead man in the dungeon. Valen grips my chin and holds me hostage. His lips brush against mine, and he smiles when I shiver.

"No need to be scared, princess," he whispers, causing me to lean in closer.

There's a feeling of safety that emanates from him. The other two have danger in their auras, whereas Valen is different, he's lighter. Lighter? I'm losing my fucking mind.

Kai is behind me, his hands on my hips, and he moves closer to murmur in my ear, "Don't be scared. You've been accepted into the family already. Now all that's left is to decide if you want to take that last step."

I don't know what to say. How do you even consider an offer like that? It's not like I didn't know it was coming, but the idea that it could happen right now, depending on my decision, is a lot to take in.

"We don't want you to feel pressured," Valen tells me.

"So you won't suffocate me?" I ask with a small smile, and a hand gently wraps around my neck.

Kai's voice is in my ear. "Not unless you ask us to."

I have no doubt they would do it, and they'd

enjoy it more than I can fathom. I haven't ever been sexually open to anything. The usual, *vanilla* lifestyle has always been enough for me. But right here and now, I realise there's so much more to explore, and if I agree to it, I'm pretty sure they'll happily teach and guide me, and I'll enjoy every moment of it. The fantasy is now becoming real. More real than I ever expected.

"I... I don't know," I respond, nervously.

Then Valen leans in close and steals my lips in a gentle kiss. He takes my hands and lowers them to my sides, and I allow him to control me. He dips his tongue into my mouth when I part my lips, and I taste him. He has a whisky flavour on his tongue, and I want to smile.

Kai's lips capture my neck, a teasing trail of warmth sends a shiver down my spine.

"I don't think the princess is going to refuse." Kai's words cause me to tremble, and I find the need to squeeze my thighs together.

As much as I'm enjoying the kiss with Valen, I can't stop my thoughts from drifting to the shower, and when I finally break away from Val, I glance over and find Judah watching. His dark, arched brow lifted, and the corner of his mouth tilted upward as he regards us.

"So, princess?" Judah questions as he sheds his briefs, and I'm gifted with the view of every inch of his body—the lean muscle and tanned skin. And even though I try not to look, I can't help noticing the size of him.

When I'm able to tear my gaze away, I look at Valen who's still waiting on my answer. I can't voice my agreement, so I nod, and his smile brightens his face when I do.

"You need to say it," Valen tells me. "If you want to stop, we stop."

His assurance calms me, somewhat, and I realise there's no turning back now. I'm with all of them. I'm going to wear Judah's ring on my finger, but I'll have made a promise to not one but all three of them. I'm not going to run away, and if I'm being honest with myself, I don't want to.

Even if I wanted to, there's no longer a reason for me to leave. I've taken the last leap into the darkness. Whatever happens next has to be easier than what I've just done.

"I'm not leaving," I finally say out loud.

"I'll help you." This comes from Valen, but it's not only him, it's Kai as well.

My clothes are gently removed from my body. There's no rush. They take their time undressing me until I'm standing before them in nothing but my panties. It's been years since I allowed anyone to see me naked. None of the guys I've been with back in England ever saw me completely bare. The scars on my body have kept me from wanting to be seen. But all three men in this room know about me now. They've seen my medical records and know about my surgery. They know I'm not perfect.

"Beautiful," Valen says softly as he takes my hand and leads me to the shower.

That's when Judah takes over, and it's the first time since I met him, that he looks almost sheepish. It doesn't last long, though, because as soon as he notices me watching him, that calm, emotionless expression reappears.

The other two guys join us moments later, and the warm spray cleans the blood from my hands and from my chest where it had splattered. Judah pulls me closer to him, my chest to his. Valen and Kai step up behind me, and I feel their toned torsos against my back. They cocoon me as if I'm fragile butterfly wanting to spread its wings. But my wings have now been clipped. As Judah leans in to press his lips gently to mine, I can't help but moan. Someone slips their hand down my body and Judah moves back before he pulls Valen in and their mouths fuse. It's one of the hottest things I've ever witnessed.

I thought I'd be afraid. But as we move together, hands and arms, mouths and tongues, it feels natural. I can't explain it.

I had my breakthrough with Judah at the party, and I've had a bond with Valen for a while, so when I turn to Kai, I can't help but smile because he's the only one I haven't truly connected with yet.

Even though we've been training together, our interactions have always been professional, but now as I stretch up on my tiptoes and place a kiss on his mouth, I can feel the vibration of his moan, rumbling through his chest.

"The princess is coming out of her cage." Judah's words wash over me, making me smile and I notice that the men have moved, and now I'm fully in Kai's arms. Judah brings Valen closer once more, and they kiss, their tongues dual and dance, while Kai's fingers slip between my thighs.

The blood has gone from our skin, from our bodies, and even though the memory will always be there, I know I'll be kept safe by these three men who want me.

Suddenly, I feel hands trailing down my hips and gripping my arse, and I'm lifted between Judah and Kai.

"What are you doing?" I ask, then a gasp falls from my lips when I feel them hard against me.

I've never been with two guys at the same time, let alone three, so this is scary, but I can't deny I'm turned on.

Fingers tease me as Judah reaches around and dips his fingers between my legs. The sensation of him teasing my clit makes me shiver, and his touch is so gentle, I can't help but groan, needing more. Kai steals my mouth in a kiss while Valen trails his lips over my neck, my shoulder, and down my arm as he lifts my hand to his mouth.

I'm being taken by three men, and I haven't ever felt safer. Kai's hands on my arse hold me steady as Judah's hand dips deeper. His fingers enter me, stretching me, and as he fucks me with two digits, I moan into Kai's mouth.

I'm dizzy from the pleasure coursing through my veins. The hot water sprays over us as we lose ourselves in each other, and I don't want to ever leave this intimate space.

Judah continues teasing and taunting me. He doesn't apply enough pressure to send me over the edge, keeping me teetering until I know I'm about to beg for more. My mind races back to the day he caught me spying. He told me I'd beg for his cock, and I'm very fucking close to it.

"When I tell you to come," Judah whispers in my ear, "I want you to actually fucking obey me. Can you do that for me, little spy?"

His words send heat racing down my spine and through my veins. All I can do is nod. We shift, and I'm so needy I can't focus on anything but the orgasm that's remained elusive since Judah started toying with me.

A hand wraps around my neck, and another

makes it's way to my pussy once more, and I'm lost to the pleasure. Suddenly, without warning, Judah is inside me. His cock, thick and hard, stretches me causing me to moan out loud.

"This time, you will do what I want you to do," he tells me as the other two watch me come apart.

Judah thrusts again and again, and I feel myself climbing closer to that edge. I want nothing more than to free-fall. There are mouths on my nipples, sucking and biting, while Judah finally takes what's his. I may have fantasised about this once before, but it's nothing like the real thing. Reality is a million times better.

"Judah!" I cry out when my clit is pinched and he slams into me one more time.

We're all so close to finding our release, and I can't stop myself from falling over the edge again. There are hands all over my body, and I'm dizzy with the pleasure slowly wracking through me. My nerve-endings tingle with an electric current so strong I'm seeing stars as my head drops back onto Judah's shoulder.

I'm not sure when they set me back down on my feet, but when I open my eyes, Kai is smiling down at me.

"You're beautiful," he tells me, and it's the gentlest I've ever heard him, but then again, most of the time we've spent together has been in the gym, fighting.

"Thank you," I murmur, slightly unsure of myself at the moment.

It's new to me, having one man look at me as if I'm the most beautiful thing in the world, but having all three of them staring at me makes me shy.

"Come," Judah says in his gruff tone and wraps me in a towel.

I didn't even notice the shower being turned off, but I'm led into the bedroom where I sit on the bed, and each of the guys take their places around my room. Kai sits in the armchair by the balcony door, while Valen leans against the dresser and Judah settles down beside me.

"This isn't easy for you," Judah tells me in the gentlest tone I've heard from him since we met. "We'll take things slowly."

"We'll take as long as you need," Valen says, but I can't concentrate with all three of them in nothing but towels, still wet from the shower and looking far too distracting.

I nod slowly, before I find the words to say, "I'm going to need some time to get used to this."

For a long, quiet moment, we sit together before Judah rises from the bed and Kai stands up from the chair. I smile at Kai, and the affection in his gaze is warming, making butterflies flutter in my belly. We took a big step together tonight, and I'm glad we did.

"We'll leave you to get dressed," Judah tells me. "Dinner will be in the dining room in thirty minutes."

I stand, and Kai leans in to press his lips to mine before he whispers, "You're incredible, sweetheart. And that's the first of many more times I intend to enjoy you."

The promise in his tone makes my body ache for more. And as I watch Kai and Judah leave, I know I'm blushing because my face is red hot. I want to call them back so they can hold me again.

Valen remains behind, and looking over at me, he smiles and says, "You're incredibly beautiful."

A blush warms my cheeks when Valen cups my face and presses his lips to mine. I lean into his warmth as his other hand grips my hip and tugs me closer.

"We need to get ready for dinner," I tell him, and I smile when he groans in frustration before stepping back. "There's the rest of our lives for this, apparently."

He chuckles, and it makes his eyes sparkle.

"Oh, I have no doubt about that, sweetheart," he says with a cheeky wink before he turns and makes his way out into the hallway, and I finally shut my bedroom door before leaning against it.

I don't regret anything that just happened, all I can think about is doing it again. Kai and Valen have burrowed themselves inside me, not just psychically, but mentally and emotionally as well. And that surprises me because I'm still fighting my feelings for Judah. I don't want to admit I want him. Even though we just had mind-blowing sex, I can't find it in my heart to fall in love with him just yet.

UP IN FLAMES

JUDAH

WHEN I TOLD BRIELLE LAST NIGHT THAT SHE HAD TO decide what to do, I expected her to run. I didn't think we'd end up fucking in the shower. The memory of her pussy taking my dick is still fresh in my mind as I wait for the other guys to get here for the meeting.

There could be repercussions when it comes to what Brielle did to DiMario, so we need to be ready. I know there'll be talk around the campus, but none of the students will come after us because the evidence is enough to convince them that Marco needed to die. Things could so easily go up in flames with the other families, though, so we need to make sure we're prepared.

The door opens and Kai saunters in. The look on his face is obvious. We've all connected with her on a deeper level, but it doesn't mean I can trust her completely. She's been welcomed into our world now, into our family, but she's still a Saviatti. One thing I do find strange is that her father hasn't tried to make contact.

"How are you after last night?" Kai settles into the chair on my right-hand side and watches for my reaction.

We're all trained to read people, looking for those small, telling nuances, but we're also trained to hide anything that could give away an inkling of information to our enemy, or indeed, to my best friend who is fishing for details.

"I'm fine."

"Come on, Jude," he says, leaning back as Valen enters the room with a smile on his face. "You can tell us."

I look at Kai, but I'm not sure what to say. As much as I want to talk about Brielle, I know it's not going to be a quick conversation, because we need to delve deeper. We took it slow with her last night, but it's not always going to be like that with three men who enjoy taking control. Her fire ignites our desire, and I know we all want nothing more than to experience it again.

"This isn't the time for that."

Just then, Jordan and Emilio walk into the room, and the subject is shut down for the time being. I know however, when we're alone it will come up again, and I'm going to have to decide how to deal with my emotions. If I'm not in control, how am I meant to keep my poise with Brielle.

"What's happening?" Jordan slumps into the chair and offers me a smirk, as if he knows something has changed. It certainly has shifted, and I'm still getting used to it.

"We need to talk about Saviatti," I finally say after giving each of them a glance. "The Agency has been following him, making sure he's staying on the right path, so to speak."

"And he's not?" Emilio asks, leaning his forearms on the table.

"He's meeting with the families who are opposed to us, and who have encroached on our territories over the years."

I open the folder with the proof and slide a printed, stapled document to each of them before sitting back and allowing them to peruse the information.

It's Emilio who looks up first and says, "Perhaps we need reinforcements."

For him to suggest this surprises me. Because it's his father we're talking about.

"You do realise if we bring in the others, there may be deadly consequences, and Brielle may end up hating all of us," I respond.

The Agency are good when it comes to

surveillance, but there is a part of their organisation that handles the more brutal side of things. If we don't want to get our names involved in something, we call on them. Most times, I want to handle things myself, but this is far too sensitive for us to deal with.

"If we tell them they need to bring him in alive, perhaps we can find a way of getting through to him," Emilio suggests, the hopeful expression on his face makes me wish there was another way, but I know Saviatti won't come here of his own accord, even with his children living on the island.

"Why don't you go to him, Emilio?" I throw out the idea that suddenly sparks in my mind. "Take Jordan, and you both go and try to talk to him. Reassure him that we won't take things further if he obeys the laws we set out for him."

"You want me to talk to a man who abandoned me and my mother, leaving us to struggle for years under the fucking Capos for no reason. He could have been there and stood up for his family!"

Emilio pushes to his feet, and I realise just how much this bothers him. He's always been indifferent about his father, so this reaction is something I didn't expect it.

"I know," I say gently, hoping to appease his frustration and anger for a moment. "I'm just hoping he'll finally step up and take responsibility for his family. Perhaps it will be helpful if you meet with him, face to face. Maybe he can explain his actions to you. Maybe give you answers to questions you didn't know you had." I sit back and look at Emilio. "It isn't going to be easy, by any means. But, if you can look past all the bullshit, this could be a way of finding out why he abandoned you and your mother, you never know."

"I'll think about it," he tells me as he glares. "I've no love lost for the arsehole, and if he thinks that me coming to him and asking him to reconsider his position is a show of affection, I will kill him."

Emilio's words have a bite of anger, and I've no doubt he means what he says. But there's also an underlying concern bothering me. Emilio wants to connect with his half-sister, but Brielle is hell-bent on loving her father. I doubt she'll ever forgive him for any wrongdoing against the old man.

Her father's not as angelic as she seems to believe. I haven't told her about the secrets he's been hiding from her, because we needed her onside before I even thought about sharing those.

"There are things going on that we hadn't even considered," Valen says. "Savatti's appears to be trying to get back into organisations he outed to the FBI, do you think the Bosses will stand for it?"

"No, they won't. You know that," I respond as I glance around the room. "Unless he's offering them something, *or someone*, that's invaluable to them. Or, he could still be working for the FBI and trying to infiltrate the families by coming back with his tail between his legs."

"He obviously wanted Brielle to be safe before doing this," Kai says. "Or maybe there's more to her being here than we thought."

"Than *you* both thought." I point at Val and Kai.

When she first arrived, they both had rose-coloured glasses on.

"Fuck off," Kai throws back. "You were just as smitten. You didn't want to admit it, though."

"What if my sister is in on this?" Emilio voices my concern, loud and clear.

It's been playing on my mind. I've told both Val and Kai my fears, but they seemed too distracted by her beauty.

It's my turn to nod as I say, "It's something I've mentioned before."

"I don't want to doubt my sister, but there's no reason for me to trust her either." Emilio has settled down again, and I'm thankful for it. I don't need someone running off the rails for any reason.

"I haven't gotten any vibe off her that she's hiding something," Valen says.

He's the one who's spent the most time with Brielle and has the closest relationship with her. My thoughts begin to drift back to last night in the shower. I'm still surprised at what happened. There's been animosity between Brielle and I since she arrived, but last night I couldn't stop myself, I wanted her to know she's ours.

"There's also the little topic she's been hiding from us."

Her medical records are clear. I didn't think we'd discover much from Marco, but when we searched his apartment, we came across his collection of files on Brielle. It seems he was working, alongside his father, to find Saviatti.

"You mean in the files from Marco?" Kai looks at me as he speaks.

Nodding, I respond, "Yeah, there are some interesting facts about her. Mainly the transplant surgery. I have a feeling it's the reason Saviatti defected."

I need to sit her down and find out just what the fuck happened. There's no information on who the donor was, and that's what I have my men looking into now, but in the meantime, I need to talk to Brielle.

"What are you talking about?" Emilio asks, and I realise he wasn't around when we went through the files. I had him out running errands, and he didn't return until late, last night.

"Marco had information on Brielle. It seems he was looking into her past. There are several folders about her life from before and after your father took her away from Italy. It seems there's much more to her story than we originally thought."

"So, she is hiding shit from all of us," Emilio bites out.

"I'm not hiding anything." Brielle's voice, coming from the doorway, surprises all of us.

All heads whip towards her, and my eyes land on the beauty who's now entering the meeting room. She's dressed in a pair of skin-tight jeans and a T-shirt that's far too big for her and is hiding her luscious curves.

"Then what are you doing?" Emilio's tone has turned to ice as he looks at his sister.

Their similarities are clear. They are family. It's just too bad they can't see it for themselves. But only time can make that happen.

I glance at my own brother for a moment, and I can see how strong our bloodline runs. Turning my attention back to the princess, I rest my hands on the arms of my chair and tip my head to the side as I regard her.

"Why don't you sit down and tell us the full story," I ask her.

I'd prefer finding out all we need to know from her, rather than having to go to her father. I doubt he'll offer up any information, especially when it comes to his daughter, but if she can't give me what I want, I will have to get it from him.

Perhaps bringing him in here and keeping him in a cell may force him to change his mind. That's what those cells are built for. They're designed to break the mind and spirit. Even those who believe they're strong, end up shattering far sooner than they'd think possible.

Brielle slips into a chair, her eyes downcast, and I want to order her to look at me, but I wait until she does it of her own accord. I realise I want her to want to look at me. We made sure she knows who owns her when we took that final step and fucked her. But, even though all three of us will be hers and she ours, she's still ultimately going to be my wife. And with that, comes the responsibility to ensure she accepts our dynamic, rather than demanding a conventional marriage.

"When I was younger, my father found out I had a heart defect," she whispers in that sweet voice of hers, but the room is so silent we can hear every word. Her confession has a captive audience.

All of us stay silent. There's nothing we can say to ease her worry, not yet anyway. We have to wait until Brielle is ready. I never expected her to burrow herself so deeply into our world. And now she has, I don't want her to leave.

"It was minor, but then I got sick one day, and a common cold turned to pneumonia. That's when I almost died. It was clear I needed a transplant. The doctors were adamant. They also explained that if I received a new heart, I'd be on immunosuppressant medication for the rest of my life. But my father didn't care and made it happen."

Her words set me on edge. I knew it was serious, but the idea of her no longer living does something to me. My feelings towards her have changed. And I don't know how to handle it.

"So he took you into the hospital?" I throw out, recalling the knowledge I garnered from her records.

"He did." She nods, and I can read the sadness in her eyes.

She doesn't look at either of us as she blinks slowly. It's as if time has slowed, and all I see is her. I didn't expect the emotions to capture me as much as they have, but here I am, ready to fall into her inferno. I knew this girl would be trouble from the moment I met her. I would kill for her now, and it wouldn't have me second-guessing my decision. I'm ready to go up in flames for her.

"And you got a transplant," I offer again, causing Emilio to glance at me before turning his attention back to his sister.

The thing is our world is about to explode. I know it, and so does Val and Kai. We've all read the information.

"I did get a donor." This time, when she speaks, her gaze lands on Emilio.

The secrets in the Saviatti family are immense. And I know Emilio is going to want to go to his father after this next revelation—there's no question about it. If I was Emilio, I'd want to face the bastard and talk to him myself. I look back at Brielle who's staring at me. No anger in her gaze, just the slight flicker of worry. She's scared of hurting her brother. She doesn't need to be, though, because it wasn't her choice at the time. It was her father's.

"They found a donor who happened to be the daughter of my father's mistress," Brielle whispers before lowering her gaze to the table. "She was about my age at the time."

Emilio is silent, and I'm not sure he's put the puzzle pieces together yet. But they'll fall into place soon enough.

"It was a perfect match," Brielle whispers. "I was sad that someone had to die for me to get better, but my father said it's how life works."

"She was your age?" Emilio's voice takes on a tone that hints at his new-found knowledge. "You mean…"

"Yes." Brielle nods slowly, taking in the man who she knows is going to lose his shit in a moment.

The chair Emilio is sitting on is pushed back, the legs scraping across the hardwood floor. His hands fist on the desk as he pins her with a glare.

"My sister died," he hisses with venom lacing his

tone. "I was told she was in an accident. I didn't know that she was a donor. Even when I was old enough, nobody told me the truth. What happened the night of the accident?"

One died. One lived.

Emilio's sister died, but she wasn't Saviatti's daughter. Emilio's mother had the baby with another man. And even though Emilio knew his sister had died, he didn't understand the intricacies of the families. He didn't know about the mafia at that stage. When a Boss needed something, they wielded their power to get what they wanted with a click of their fingers. And it seems, that's what Brielle's father did.

"I don't know what happened that night. I was just told that a heart had been found, and I was taken into surgery."

Brielle's eyes plead with her brother for understanding as she pushes to her feet and places a hand on his. It's the most I've seen them interact since they met. He doesn't pull away, but he glares at her.

"There are so many things our father has kept from us. But none of it's my fault," she says as she looks at Emilio.

I'm pretty sure it's the first time they've spoken more than a few words to each other. Since Brielle arrived, they've been civil to each other, but the connection just hasn't been there.

I get it.

But it can't go on like it is, because there won't be much future for us in this house if she can't accept him, and he her. Within these walls, our family is tight-knit, and I don't want anyone feeling as if they don't fit in.

In a house of misfits, we're a solid family unit, loyal and accepting. Unless someone pushes us beyond our limit, of course. Like Marco.

"It's not your fault," Emilio says, his eyes flicking to each of us at the table before landing back on Brielle. "I'm leaving tomorrow for the mainland. I'll go to our father, and he'll have to face me. I want answers, and I won't leave without them."

"You realise what you may have to do?" I ask, ignoring Brielle's scrutiny.

I can feel her gaze boring into me like a fucking drill, but I don't want her to see what's going through my mind. And I have a feeling she'll read me if I look directly at her.

"I do." Emilio nods and waits for my response.

I prefer it when the Princes are on the grounds of the mansion. But I know Emilio needs to see his father. He needs answers, and I'm not about to deny him those. It's the only way to get closure.

"I agree," I finally say, and I see his shoulders sag in relief.

"I'll let you know how things go," Emilio responds.

"Don't hurt him," Brielle whispers, looking at her brother.

I can't imagine what it's like, knowing your father is a lying bastard. But then again, he saved her life.

"He made sure that part of my sister will live on in you," Emilio says as he stares at Brielle. "He didn't tell me, but neither did my mother, so I'm not only blaming him."

"No one will get hurt, Brielle, unless our hands are forced and a difficult decision has to be made, but if it does come to the worst, you'll be able to say your goodbyes." I keep my tone calm as I speak.

"Why do you persist in being such a cold-hearted bastard?" she asks.

I almost laugh out loud at her question. She'll soon learn who I truly am. And it will be eye-opening.

The office door flies open and one of the up-and-coming Capos for the Brindisi clan rushes in with two of my guards behind him. He's just taken on the role from his predecessor who was tortured and killed in the middle of town.

This may be an island with a university, students, and teachers, but it's also a place the Bosses can come to finish their dirty work without needing to pay off the police.

"I'm sorry, Judah," he tells me as he tries to catch his breath. "Something has happened."

I'm on my feet and glaring at him. "Well, spit it out, I'm busy here."

"I've overheard there's a plan to take down the whole of Black Hollow." He looks like he's seen a fucking ghost. There have been threats in the past. Too many to count, but this has my blood running cold.

"Call a meeting, and bring in every fucking Capo there is. I want it done tonight." He's out the door, following my order, and I know that soon enough, all hell is about to break loose.

LOVE IS A WEAPON

KAI

I DIDN'T THINK ABOUT THE FUTURE WITH A WOMAN until Brielle entered our lives. I took each day as it came, and I never expected an emotion as strong as love to take a hold of me. But now things have changed, and I'm unsure of my place with her. I don't know how she feels about me. With Valen and Judah, I know how we feel about each other. Brielle is an anomaly.

My focus is not on work. The classes I have coming up are going to be a challenge because the only thing on my mind is her. She's in my thoughts, and I'm not sure how to get her out. But then again...

Do I want her out?

"Kai," Brielle's voice steals my attention, bringing me back to the present, where I'm standing in the gym with my cock throbbing at the idea of her laid bare between the three of us.

"What are you doing here?" I demand.

I didn't expect her to be here. Not that I'm complaining. She looks incredible in a summer dress that's the colour of cherries. The hemline hits her mid-thigh, while the strap top is offering up delicious views of her shoulders and those gorgeous curves of her cleavage.

"I think we need to talk at some point," she tells me with a shy smile. "I mean… You've seen me naked."

"I have," I agree with a nod. "And what a fucking delicious vision that was." I cross my arms as she enters the workout space.

I've been in here with her so many times, training her to fight, but this feels a little different than before. Or rather, it feels far more intimate this time.

"I just thought if you're class isn't starting for a while, maybe I can sit with you and we can talk." Her cheeks heat as she glances around the room, but she doesn't look at me.

"Are you shy?" My question makes her smile, but then she nods slowly.

After all that's happened between us, I can't help but feel protective towards her. I step closer, and I reach for her chin. Gently, I tip her head back so she's looking at me.

"You know you can tell me anything." I whisper gently.

"I've never had three men who are so focused on me." Her admission makes me pull her into my arms. This is one of the few times I've been alone and close to her, other than when we've been training.

"Look at me," I order, taking the lead. When she obeys, something deep inside me comes to life. "You're ours. It doesn't matter which one of us is with you. There's no reason to hide. You should see us all as the same person in your life—lover, protector, friend." I glance at my watch. "My next class starts in about forty minutes." I tell her. "So, we've got time to sit down and talk for a while."

Brielle nods and settles on one of the mats, crossing her legs, Buddha style. I try not to allow my gaze to trail over her exposed thighs, but I fail miserably.

"I've never been with three men," she says right off the bat, and I can't help but smile. "I mean...I haven't even been with two men at the same time, so this is all new to me."

"Okay," I respond slowly, unsure of where she's going with this. I settle opposite her, and once again, fight the desire to stare at her smooth, slender legs. "Maybe this is where you need to breathe and consider that your future is with us. Perhaps having us all here to talk to would help. Also, I know, Judah is going to be your—"

"My husband," she cuts in. "I know. I just

needed… well… I'm not sure what the hell I need. But with him, I feel this pressure to be someone that he expects me to be."

"And you're not." I nod.

Judah has this way with people. He enjoys challenging them. He's done it to all of us over the years. But I suppose, we've become accustomed to him being an arsehole.

"I think I just need to connect with you since Valen and I are already friends, at least, that's how I see him. But with you…I know nothing about you."

Her words falter, and the silence hangs heavily between us. I didn't want to tell her yet, but I think it's come time to finally admit what the fuck is going on with me and my life.

"So…" I sit back and watch her as she stares at me. "I've never known my biological parents. When I was a kid, I lived in a children's home until I was adopted. I'm not born into any of the families." She looks at me with shock at my admission. "I grew up with a last name that wasn't mine from birth. However," I pause for a moment, "I did have to accept my position within the family when I was adopted."

"What does that mean?"

"Within any organisation, there's an initiation—"

For this next bit, I need to calm myself, but I don't know how, so I push to my feet and stand. I can't sit down and have her look at me with pity. I can't have her face me when I tell her the rest.

I turn away, and focus on the gloves I need to get ready. I can feel Brielle move as she rises as well. Thankfully, I wasn't looking when she pushed to her feet, or I may have been presented with a view that would have distracted me from the conversation.

"Tell me," Brielle whispers gently from behind me.

I half expect her to touch me, to place a hand on my shoulder, but I'm thankful she doesn't. For this, I need space.

"I was five when I was adopted," I start as I go back in my mind.

Most of it is blurry now. There aren't many things I willingly recall from those days. I've buried so many memories, but I can't fight the ones that resurface from time to time. As much as I'd like to.

I leave the silence hanging between us for a long while. I don't want to fill it unnecessarily. And I know that when I do tell my story, she'll turn and run in the opposite direction.

"I wasn't worried about my adoption because I hated living in the children's home for many reasons that I'll share with you at another time. I was told that the family I was going to live with was rich and influential in the town. But for me, the most important thing they could do was put clothes on my back and give me a comfortable bed to sleep in."

There'd been so many nights in the children's home when I prayed someone would want me. But each morning arrived, and I was still alone, still in the home. Day in and day out, couples would visit the home to adopt a kid, but no one ever chose me.

Until he walked in.

"When I first saw the man who'd come to adopt me, I thought he was the coolest person ever. Dressed in a black pinstripe suit, a button-up shirt, and shoes that shone so bright, even in the dim light of our cafeteria."

"He was the Boss?" Brielle asks slowly, already noting where this story is going.

I nod. "Yeah," I tell her. "He was the Boss. He was best friends with Judah's Dad. Over the years, the Veniers and Erranis have claimed nearly half the country. The Errani family rule over the middle of Italy, and the Veniers have the South, including Sicily. Here I was, a nobody. And the Boss of the Errani family chose me."

"So that would be Michele Errani?" Brielle asks, which has me turning to finally face her.

"It is," I confirm. "And as much as I wish the bastard was dead, he's still alive and well. Kicking and fighting whoever disagrees with him."

"What happened after he adopted you?"

She's completely and utterly immersed in my past, and as uncomfortable as it is to share my story, I realise, she needs this. For her to fully accept all of us, she's going to need to know who we are.

The more we divulge about our pasts, the more Brielle will trust us. And even though there are still dark secrets we all keep hidden for our own mental health, the time has come for us to share what we can.

"For years, I was taught that love is a weapon, and we should wield it with strength and grace, but also, not allow the emotion to swallow us up," I tell her.

I shake my head when I consider what I've done in the past. I never wanted to get into a serious relationship before because I knew I'd have to explain who I am. With Judah and Valen, they get it. They've been in this life as long as I have, longer even, but with Brielle coming into it now, it's not the same thing at all.

"That's not the way to look at life. Or at love," Brielle says. Her surprise is clear in her tone.

Nodding slowly, I shrug before continuing, "For the first few years, I believed what I was taught. It's something I had to do in order to survive this life. So I did. But when I was nine, it was time for me to be taken into the family, formally. Not legally. The paperwork had already been done in relation to my adoption, but now it was time for me to learn who I was going to become."

"And you had to kill someone," Brielle guesses as she looks at me with concern dancing in those pretty eyes.

The only other people who know about this, besides my father, are Judah and Valen. Not even Emilio or Jordan know this secret about me.

"I did," I confirm with a nod.

This time, there is a weighted silence that hangs like a guillotine. The blade precarious as it waits to be dropped. I don't know what she'll make of me after this. Brielle may never want to talk to me again, and if I was being honest with myself, I wouldn't want to either.

But there's nothing more I want right now, than for her to look at me and tell me she'll still care for me after what I'm about to tell her.

"He brought me into this room, where I was sat in the dim light. His men dragged a body in behind them, and I was convinced whoever it was had been killed already. I actually felt relief, but then they bound the body to a chair, and it was only when they woke her up that I realised who she was."

Brielle's gaze widens in surprise, her mouth pops open, and I know she's probably figured it out. But she doesn't say anything, she allows me to continue.

After a deep breath, I say, "When I looked into

this woman's eyes, I knew who she was. She didn't even have to open her mouth."

This time, her voice is nothing more than a soft shaky breath. "It was your birth mother."

I want to say no, I want to shake my head and tell her she's wrong, but I can't, because she isn't. That night, I changed. I turned off all those feelings that had been plaguing me for years, and I became the emotionless soldier my adopted father wanted me to be.

"And you did what was expected of you?" Brielle questions as she glances up at me.

I can tell she already fears the worst, even though hope of a happier ending to my story still glimmers in her eyes, but she doesn't need to hold onto that useless emotion. I dispensed with it a long time ago.

"I had no choice. It was made clear that it was either me pulling the trigger or I would have to watch them torture her. Michele wanted me to learn what this life was truly like. He told me I could watch her learn her lesson for walking out on me, or I could end her pain, quickly and easily."

"So he used your mother, who you didn't even know was alive, as a weapon," Brielle puts the pieces together, and when she blinks, a tear trickles down her cheek, forcing me to rush to her.

"Don't," I tell her as I swipe her cheek. "There's no need to cry." I don't want her tears. It's a fucked-up situation, and I hate seeing her like this. "I'm telling you about my past only because you need to know who I am."

"And now that I do, I feel…"

"Pity?"

She shakes her head. "Sadness."

I pull her into my arms and cocoon her from the darkness I've just spilled all over her sunshine. I don't need her to ever feel sadness for me. Even though my life started out filled with violence, I've become stronger for it. I don't regret anything, but I do wish I could change how people see me.

Knowing I killed my own mother to show her mercy, softened the guilt. Michele made me a soldier that day, and in some ways, I'm thankful for it.

"Is that one of the reasons you consider yourself lawless?" she whispers against my chest, and I take a step back to look her in the eye.

"Yes," I admit. "But I'll never kill someone who is innocent again. That was the first and last time I ever did that. Granted, she wasn't entirely innocent, but she didn't deserve what happened to her. She was an absent mother, not a criminal."

Brielle nods. "I get it. But you can't ever blame yourself for what you did."

"Oh," I say as the corner of my mouth tips upwards. "Trust me, darling, I don't blame myself.

It's Michele's doing. And he'll get what's coming to him soon enough."

There are so many working parts to this, but I can't tell her those yet, because they involve more than just me. She doesn't know the rest of the story, and it's best I keep it that way for now. Judah and Valen need to be present when we tell her the plan. Then we can finally move on.

I never wanted to be the Boss of the family, the clan. But I know Michele has named me the next in line, his successor. It won't be long until I get there. And when I do, I'll make sure his work ethic—all the rules he impressed upon us, his soldiers, are scrapped.

"Now," I say as I look at Brielle. "We've had a bit of a chat about me, but there's more I need to know about you. I'm sure Judah and Valen will also need to be there for that, so if you can wait until tonight, maybe we can all sit down together and come clean about our secrets."

"I'd like that," she tells me. "I never meant to keep anything from anyone. Especially you, Val, and Jude. I've just been taught to hide the real story about my transplant. My father didn't want anyone to know. And he didn't tell me who the donor was. I found out by snooping."

"So, you are a little spy," I tell her as I smile. Her cheeks darken with a soft pink, which makes me chuckle. "Don't be embarrassed by it. You should be proud that your skills are so good you're able to do it unnoticed."

Brielle shrugs. "I just needed to know what my father had been hiding from me. I don't like secrets, and he's obviously got so many. I just didn't realise how deep they truly went. And now I do…"

I wonder, if faced with the same decision, whether Brielle would be able to do what I did, all those years ago. It's not easy to kill anyone, let alone a parent. Brielle grew up with her father, whereas I didn't know my mother.

To me she was a stranger. Perhaps that's what made it a easier. That moment I pulled the trigger changed me—I became closed off, but it didn't alter the fact that I believe women should be cherished.

No woman should have a man raise his hands to her. And I will die upholding that moral code that has been instilled in me since I was far too young to understand it. None of the men I've grown up around consider it wrong to harm a woman. Besides Judah and Valen, of course, and I know Emilio and Jordan are of the same mindset, which is one of the reasons we're all so close.

We may be the Lawless Princes, but that doesn't mean we've broken all the rules.

"Will you be okay till tonight?" I ask Brielle.

She smiles so brightly, it makes my fucking chest

tighten. I didn't expect her to affect me like this, but without realising it, she's dug her nails deep inside my chest.

"I will," she tells me with a nod. "I think I'm going to finish up some of my projects that are due in a few weeks. If I can get ahead, it will help me focus."

"Good plan. Getting in front with your work will make the courses a lot easier. That's what I did. And when you're ready, we'll work some more on your fighting skills. Now you'll be taking over the Venier family, alongside Judah, you'll need to know it all."

"I can't wait."

When Brielle first arrived here, I never once expected her to feel this way about the life laid before her, but I think everything has changed. Something's clicked, and now she's ours.

"And we'll all have dinner tonight," I tell her.

Emilio is leaving for the mainland, and Jordan will no doubt be out with any one of a number of girls he frequently has on his arm. So it will be just the four of us, and tonight will be something of a confession circle.

"I'd like that," Brielle replies. "Thank you for telling me about yourself. I know you didn't have to open up, but I cherish your honesty. It means a lot to me."

"You'll always get honesty from the Princes, even if you don't want it. It's something we agreed amongst ourselves, years ago. We've all grown up with lies, and we don't believe they bring anything but destruction."

"See you later," Brielle says as she leaves me with my thoughts.

I'll have a class of students here soon, and as much as I'd rather spend the afternoon with her, I know I'm going to have to focus.

I feel good, lighter, now she knows.

I just hope we can move forward after dinner tonight when all those hidden truths will be revealed. No more lies, and no more fucking secrets.

NEVER SURRENDER

BRIELLE

It's almost dinner time, but my mind is still on what Kai told me about his past. It can't be easy living with the reminder that you killed your mother.

With all the secrets slowly making themselves known, I feel as if I'm spinning in the dark, and bits of light keep blinding me. Never did I think I'd come to care for these men. Each of them broken in some way. Which has me worried about what Valen's story is.

When I make my way into the dining room, the three of them are there already, waiting on me. Nerves flutter in my belly as I glance at each one, their eyes focused on me. I'm pretty sure they know I've spoken with Kai and he's admitted to his past.

"Join us," Judah tells me as he leans back in this chair at the head of the table.

To his right, there's an empty seat, and beside

that, Valen sits with a small smile on his face. To Judah's left is Kai.

They're all dressed in button-up shirts, no ties, but each one looks incredibly handsome. I settle in the chair that Judah points to, the one between him and Valen.

"Did you have a good day?" Judah questions as he flicks those hazel eyes my way.

"Yes, it was eye-opening," I respond, allowing my eyes to dance towards Kai. He offers me a smile, and a slight nod before I look back at Judah. "I think it was much needed after everything that's come to light."

"And you're not afraid," Judah says, which confirms that Kai has told him what he shared with me. I'm glad he has because I don't want any more secrets.

"Why would I be?" I look at Judah.

He shrugs. "Most women would be. This isn't an easy life, especially when you're not used to it. Violence isn't exactly a choice you make. Being part of the organisation doesn't allow many freedoms."

"There are few choices in this life, and I've come to terms with it, Judah. I'm not a child," I throw back. "But the truth is, I don't want to run anymore. I'm tired of hiding."

"Then there will be no more hiding," Judah says.

"You now know Kai's story. And soon, you'll learn Valen's."

I look over at the man in question, and he offers a nod. With the wedding getting closer each day, I know I'm going to need to learn all there is to know about my fiancé as well. I doubt it's going to be all good, but whatever happens, I know I'm in this forever.

There is no escaping what was set in motion years ago. The families are strict about contracts, and my name sits on one where my father gave me away to the Veniers.

Just then, two of the staff I've come to know, over my time being here, walk in with steaming plates of food in hand. They set down all the serving dishes, along with shiny silver spoons. It smells delicious, and my stomach agrees with a soft rumble.

I haven't eaten since this morning, so I'm ready to devour anything put in front of me. The amount of pasta on the table is shocking. With only four of us, I'm pretty sure a lot of it will go to waste. I hope the staff is able to enjoy any leftovers.

Three different serving bowls, filled to the brim with a variety of tagliatelle, spaghetti, and penne dishes, sit in front of me. Also placed on the table is garlic bread that fills the room with a buttery, herby fragrance, and there's a smaller bowl containing gnocchi, one of my favourites.

I haven't felt so relaxed in a long time. Judah takes my plate and dishes a spoonful of everything onto it. Once my plate is full, the guys fill their own plates. Then red wine is poured for each of us, and the peppery, fruity flavour bursts on my tongue when I take my first sip.

"Are you enjoying your studies?" Judah asks me, capturing my attention.

In the soft candlelight, his eyes shimmer with flecks of green in the soft brown.

"I am. I didn't think I would fit in when I first arrived, because I don't really come from this life, but it's been eye-opening to discover that not everyone here is dangerous."

"Even after Marco," Kai adds.

Nodding, I sit back and recall that night. "It could have happened anywhere. He wanted more than I was willing to offer, and when he found out I was living here and promised to Judah, I think maybe he snapped."

"There was too much information about you in his apartment for his interest in you to have been random. It's obvious he'd been researching you for some considerable time," Judah tells me.

I didn't know this. They'd mentioned he had folders containing details of my life, but I didn't realise he'd been collecting information about me for months, maybe longer.

"So, you think he knew I was coming to Black Hollow all along?" I look at Judah, my food now forgotten as I wonder if someone's been watching Papa and me and for how long.

We could have been in harm's way all these years. Spies could have been keeping an eye on us, and we were none the wiser.

"We don't know what to think. We just need you to be aware that not everyone on this island is a friend." Valen's tone takes on a more serious rumble. He's always been the fun one, laughing and joking with me, so for him to be so serious, sets me on edge. "But we are here," he reassures me, taking my hand.

I'm convinced each of these men can read my mind. It's as if they're burrowing their way into my psyche, and I know I won't ever be able to get them out.

"I know," I say then. "And I can fight as well. I'm just worried about what will happen in the future. I never thought I'd be safe forever, but there's this niggle in the back of my mind that tells me a war is coming."

"It is," Judah confirms with a confident nod. "Once I step into my father's position on my birthday, there are many families who will try to overthrow me. And, as my wife, that means you'll be right by my side. Which is why I need you to be ready to take on anyone that may come at you."

The thought of having to go to war over some family name, over who is in control, makes me anxious. I don't like the old world mentality. It worked back then, but this is the present day, we're not living in the nineteen hundreds anymore.

"I will fight alongside you. One thing my father taught me is to never surrender," I tell them proudly.

I've never allowed anyone to take advantage of me, and I have never been a pushover. It's not in my nature, and I don't intend to show weakness now. I've had to take medication daily to ensure I live a long life. I was given a second chance, and I don't intend on wasting it. I'm used to fighting. Giving up is not a choice, I want to get through this. I have to.

"Then we won't have a problem," Kai says. "I didn't think you'd sit back and let anything just happen to you."

There's pride in his tone. The only other person who's ever spoken to me like that or made me feel valued is Papa, and now he's not with me anymore, I'm going to have to tell myself I'm strong.

"I was taught to fight for what I want."

"And what is it you want now, Brielle?" Judah tests me, his hazel eyes landing on mine, boring a hole right into my soul.

There's something about the way he looks at me that tells me all those things I would rather have kept hidden are no longer a secret.

"I want to live a happy life," I tell him. "I want you, Kai, and Valen safe, and I want Emilio and Jordan safe. But I also want my father to live a long and happy existence. And when he finally takes his last breath, I hope it's not because he was killed."

It's the most honesty I've offered, other than telling them about my transplant. I received a heart from the girl who, I later learnt, was the daughter of my father's mistress. The accident that took her life happened at the same time I was on the transplant waiting list. They didn't have any hope for me. I was admitted into hospital with no prospects of surviving, and then, a miracle happened.

But now I don't know if I can believe it was merely fate. Serendipity doesn't occur randomly in our world of violence and vows. There's never a magical cure for anything.

"You do know that your father may not survive the next few days," Judah tells me coldly.

"Do you have to be such a bastard?"

"No," he says with a shake of his head. "I'm being honest. Giving you the truth rather than tiptoeing around the bullshit that everyone else will offer. If you ever want the truth from anyone, the men around this table will be the ones to give it to you."

He sets down his fork and knife and looks directly at me. There's an icy chill that races down my spine when he does this. I know there's more to it than just him being honest. I can tell he's trying to connect. Previously, he would have just thrown out something hurtful and moved on, but there's been a bond formed between us now, and I don't think it's ever going to be severed.

The door to the dining room opens and four men walk in, all dressed in black. Their focus is on me, but Judah pushes to his feet and they halt all movement.

"What is this about?" he asks, his tone calm, but there's an underlying threat that seems to linger in every word he utters.

"We need to take the girl," one of the men tells Judah. "It's not in our hands anymore. And it's not in yours."

"She's my property," Judah hisses, his hands slamming down on the table in a loud thud that has me jumping in shock. "She will not leave this fucking property. If anyone comes for her, they'll be coming for the Veniers, the Erranis, and the Medicis as well." The three strongest names in the mafia.

But the men who entered are undeterred as they stare down Judah. Then Kai and Valen both rise to their feet, and I feel as if I'm a fragile princess—it annoys me. I'm far from weak.

I stand and step out from behind Valen who's been trying to hide me.

"What is this about? Who wants me?" I ask,

keeping my voice neutral, and I'm thankful they can't hear it shaking with worry.

There are too many people out there who may want me dead, but I'm not going to sit back and have the three men in my life watch me show any form of fragility.

My father, along with Kai, Valen, and Judah, taught me that surrender is futile. I'll fight, even if it ultimately brings my death.

"Your father has upset a lot of people," one of the men says.

The intruders all look like they should be doormen at a nightclub with their large bulk and broad shoulders. The one has a scar running from his left eye down to his mouth, and I can't help but shiver when I take in his face.

"This is a private residence," Judah tells them as he steps forward and pushes me behind him with his hand. But I know he can't protect me. These men won't stop now. They're here for a reason, and they're not going to leave until they've got me in their custody. "I didn't know the FBI had started hiring thugs," Judah says with a smile, and my mouth pops open.

"You don't need to know anything," Scarface says. "The only thing that matters is that the girl comes with us."

He looks at me, his stare cold and menacing. It

slices through me, causing me to shiver in fear. I've always been stronger than this, not showing others what I'm feeling, but right now, this man has me in a chokehold. He's obviously trained to see through people.

"Trust me when I say, I'm not one to bow down to anyone. My friends here will bear witness to that. So, if you would like to sit down and tell me why you stormed into our home and disturbed a lovely dinner, then you're welcome to. But you won't be leaving with anyone," Judah tells them.

I'm not sure what the hell is going on, so many thoughts are racing through my mind, but then I notice Judah's imperceptible movement. It's a sleight of hand, like a magician performing his most famous trick, and seconds later, there are shots ringing in my ears.

I can't stop the scream that escapes my lips as I'm pushed to the floor. A body covers me, but there's only so much protection Judah can offer as he and the other guys engage in a frenzied gunfight. Something hits my leg, and the agonising sting of the bullet slicing through my flesh makes me dizzy. I've never been shot at before, let alone hit with a bullet.

"Stay down," Judah tells me.

In the next second, he's gone, and I find myself alone, holding onto my leg. The thick, crimson fluid oozing from my wound covers my hands, and once again, I'm stained with someone's blood. Only this time, it's mine.

This is my life now, and I can't escape it. I shut my eyes so tight, I see sparks behind my lids. The violence makes me anxious, even though I've taken a life. This shouldn't faze me, but it does.

I try to shift to find Kai or Valen or Judah, but all I see are men in black. Some fall to the ground with heavy thuds, while others duck behind furniture, their guns expelling bullets. I can't see who they're aiming at, all I can hear are groans and shouts.

Fear skitters down my spine for the men I've come to care about. I don't want them to be hurt. I'm still not sure who sent these mercenaries, but they're here to complete a job.

My heart slams against my chest, making it difficult to breath. The cacophony in my ears is deafening. Another two men in black fall to the ground and then I see Valen gripping one of them around the neck, he's using him as a shield, and for a moment, the uneasy feeling calms somewhat. But I still can't see the other men, and I don't know if they've been shot.

It occurs to me, if I can get out of the room, I can try to find some soldiers on the property to help. I can't walk, though, because my leg feels as if it's about to explode with the pain shooting through it. Even if I could stand, there's every chance I'd get hit again, so I decide the only way to get to safety and call for help is to crawl.

Bullets continue to fly past me as I drag myself along the smooth wooden floorboards, trying to get away. But before I can get too far, I'm grabbed around the waist and hoisted up by a pair of thick, rough hands, forcing a scream to escape my lungs.

The man carrying me rushes for the patio doors, but then I feel him lunge forward as he begins to lose his balance, and I brace myself for the crash through the glass doors. I think he's been shot, but I can't be sure. I'm slammed to the ground, the thud against the cold concrete, knocking the breath from my lungs as I'm dragged outside by one ankle.

I bite down on my lip to keep from screaming in agony as I use my wounded leg to kick at the scarred face of the man who's trying to keep hold of me. Finally, a scream breaks free from my lips as I kick once more, hitting him in the jaw, and his hand releases my foot. But I'm in too much pain to get away. I roll over, hoping to locate Judah, Valen, or Kai in the melee.

And that's when I see him…

I watch as Kai comes up behind the man with the scar, and I look on in fascinated horror as he takes a sleek cable and wraps it around the oaf's large neck and tugs tight. I've never seen violence like this before. Not even in the cinema.

The wire cord doesn't look like it could do too much damage, but it does. It cuts into the flesh, slicing slowly but surely, as if the neck of this man was nothing more than butter with a hot blade slipping through it easily. But it's also Kai's strength that shocks me. I knew he worked out and provided the training for all the up-and-coming soldiers, but watching him in action for real is very different.

Blood spurts from the neck of the man Kai has in a stranglehold, and it doesn't take him long to gurgle his last breath and fall to the ground.

"Are you okay, princess?" Kai is by my side, lifting me into his arms.

He carries me into the dining room that looks like a hurricane has been through it. More of Judah's men are here now—more soldiers, Capos, and even a few of Kai's students.

"We're at war," Judah declares as he walks up to us, his hazel eyes hard and cold as they land on me.

I don't want to hear what he's going to say next, but I know I don't have a choice. Something has happened. Something I prayed would never come.

And then he says it…

"Your father has started something he's never going to be able to finish."

UNRIVALLED DESIRE

KAI

"You're hurt," Judah says as he looks at me while I'm working on Brielle. "I'll get—"

"I'm fine." I tell Judah who's staring at the wound in my side.

It's not fatal. He doesn't need to worry, but he always does. That's the reason I fucking love this man so much. He and Valen have always been by my side, and I could never live in a world without either of them. And now Brielle is a part of our dynamic.

"You're going to need stitching," Judah says. "I'll do it." We've all been trained in how to deal with injuries. It's important to know how to fix any wound in our line of work. More importantly, how to get a bullet out. "Sit down, let Valen work on Brielle's leg."

Sighing, I settle beside our girl and allow Jude to take control of the situation. The pain of the bullet is taking its toll on me, and I know I'm going to have to allow him to remove the fucker. I lie back as Valen gets to work on Brielle, and I wince when Judah makes a small incision around the bullet entry site. I've been through this so many times before, but it never gets any easier.

"Everyone out," Judah announces loudly, ordering the men to leave, his tone filled with ice. "I want the grounds thoroughly searched. Do not leave any stone unturned. If there are more intruders, I want them found and brought to the dungeon."

Judah lifts the tweezers from my wound, having captured the bullet between the prongs. The clink of metal hitting metal when he drops it into the bowl beside him echoes around us. And then, the stitches start. Thankfully, I don't need too many.

Once I'm all fixed up, I'm on my feet and worried about our princess. I'm thankful she hasn't been hurt badly, and when she looks up at me with that sparkling gaze, my chest tightens.

Once we have our privacy, Judah moves to the windows, shutting us in the dimly lit room as Valen finishes up working on Brielle's leg. A soft gasp from her lips as my fingertips brush up her inner thigh makes me smile. The pain from the wound must be horrific for her, but I wonder if we could distract her in some way.

"How are you feeling?" I whisper as I lean in to

press my lips to hers. It's a gentle feather of a kiss, and it makes her tremble.

"It hurts some, but I'm alive," she tells me. "You're worse off than I am."

I chuckle. "I'm a big boy, I'll be okay."

A quick glance at Valen is evidence enough that he has the same idea of distraction in mind. He scoots up on the table next to Brielle and pulls her into his arms. She's no longer shaking, which is a good sign.

Judah joins us, a glass of water in hand.

"Drink this," he commands Brielle who accepts without question. She must be in shock still because she doesn't argue with him. It's the first time I haven't seen them at odds. He takes the glass once she's done and sets it down. "Do you want to go to bed?"

"Please," she replies in a whisper.

Valen takes the lead and scoops her up. We move through the wreckage and make our way upstairs to her room. Val sets her down on the bed that's large enough for us all to fit. I sit at her feet and help her out of her clothes. The leggings are discarded to the floor, but her panties stay on. The lacy material is tight against her pussy, and it has my cock throbbing to be inside her again.

Judah is on her left, and as he looks at her, I can finally see the affection he feels for her. I've witnessed him look at me and Valen like that, but never Brielle. Then, he smirks as he pulls her in for a kiss.

I settle on the bed, making sure to keep pressure off the wound, and I spread Brielle's legs wide, so I can run my nose along her inner thigh. The bite of pain from my side doesn't even register when I lean in to lap at her underwear, teasing her cunt through the thin material.

She smells like heaven and tastes like sin.

Valen's mouth captures her one nipple while Judah sucks on the other. She's nothing more than a pliable vessel for us to enjoy. When Valen's mouth pops off Brielle's nipple, he shifts towards me, and pushing to my knees, I offer him my tongue, to taste our girl.

As Judah deepens our kiss, I feel a hand on my cock as he strokes me until I'm throbbing, needing to be inside anyone at this point. Pleasure races through my veins when I am pressed between Brielle's slender thighs. Judah's hand guides the head of my cock to her entrance, and as I inch into her tightness, I can't stop the moan of bliss that rumbles in my chest.

Valen sucks on her tongue as her wet, slick walls take me in. Judah releases me slowly, and his hand trails up my ribs and grips my neck. Our mouths fuse as Brielle's whimpers gets louder. My hips slam into her and Valen groans, causing me to break contact with Judah. We both turn to see her lips wrapping around Valen's hard cock.

Our bodies are connected, the three of us, along with our princess. Judah moves so he's kissing his way down my chest, all the way to where I'm connected to Brielle's perfect cunt. His tongue teases me each time I pull out. I reach for his arse, squeezing it hard, while he sucks on her clit the moment my cock slides out and then releases her when I thrust back in. I'm so lost to pleasure. My nerves feel as if they've sparked to life. It's as if I've been electrocuted, and I can't stop the euphoria from sweeping through me.

The sounds in the room are erotic and sensual, and when I look down at Valen, I can tell he's close as he fists his hands. Brielle's mouth is working him into a frenzy.

"Fuck," he groans, the deep growl making my own cock throb inside her.

Judah moves to my mouth once more, and kisses me, my fingers tease his cock gently as we twist our tongues together. The flavour of Brielle's sweet juices on his lips makes my cock thicken. I'm so close.

"Fill her up, Kai," Judah tells me. "Fill that pretty little cunt, and then I'm going to lick her clean."

His filthy words have me falling over the edge, and I can't stop from spilling my release deep in her tight pussy. When I slowly slip from her body, Judah moves between her thighs, only to lap at the wetness dripping from her.

Seeing him enjoy our combined arousal is a sight that I want to replay in my mind over and over again. It's sexy and erotic, and I move to Brielle's side, allowing her to taste us on my cock.

Like a good fucking girl, she cleans me with that pretty little tongue. I know I'll be able to go again, very fucking soon.

But for now, I watch as she swallows Valen's release. and when she cries out, I know Judah has sent her over the edge.

IN THE DARK

JUDAH

Two weeks later

WHEN THE PAPERWORK FIRST ARRIVED I DIDN'T THINK anything of it, but when I opened the email, I realised there's much more to our little princess than meets the eye.

With all the shit that's gone down in the past few weeks, I expected there to be no more secrets between us. But now I've discovered there's another small one she conveniently forgot to mention… unless she really didn't recognise him, but deep down, I don't believe that. There's no way she didn't remember the face of the man she fucked only three years ago. Even the thought of it sends me into a raging fit. But I tamp it down.

For now, I need to focus on the task at hand, and

it has nothing to do with Brielle. Her father, yes, but not her.

Brielle is strong. More so than we all imagined. My father taught me to read people, yet I failed to see the truth behind those pretty fucking eyes—more so than I have with anyone else before. I didn't think it would come to this, but now I know the whole truth, I realise I was right all along. I should have trusted my instincts. I'm glad I got to watch her make her first kill, though. I didn't think she'd be able to do it, but she surprised us all. It was refreshing to see.

We're still searching for Saviatti. Emilio nearly had him, but he escaped with the help of his connections. We'll find the bastard. He sent those arseholes into my world and they fucked it up completely. Brielle's and Kai's injuries weren't serious. It's clear these arseholes have no idea how to aim, and I'm thankful for that.

I didn't expect to want to save her, protect her, as much as I do. Even though she's to marry me, I never thought I could feel anything for her. But she's burrowed her pretty little hands into my chest and gripped my heart.

This isn't love.

It's far more volatile than that.

It's a dark obsession. I want to see her crying and begging for me to fuck her. There's no denying the chemistry between the four of us when we fuck, but tonight will be different.

Before I even consider going to her, to them, I need to sort this shit out. I walk into the dungeons and find the captured bastard bound to a chair.

It's been a long while since I was allowed to play with knives. And when I pick up my favourite blade, I smile as his eyes widen.

"Look, Judah, I don't know anything about what Marco was doing," he tells me as fear drips from his words. "If I did, I would have come to you. You know me. You've known me for years. I wouldn't defect on you," he's spouting lies. I can see them written all over his face. I don't think he'll be making it out of here alive, which is fine—for me at least.

"I'm not concerned about Marco right now. I need to know about Saviatti." I take a step towards him, and I notice him flinch, right before he tips his head in fake confidence.

I know it's all an act. We're taught how to protect ourselves, how to hide things, how to counterattack with both words and actions.

"I don't know where he is."

"You know that's a lie," I throw back as I place the tip of steel right between his legs. "If you continue to lie to me, I'm going to have to do something drastic." I twist the knife handle, causing the weapon to cut through the thick, denim material of his jeans.

He shakes his head, but I know he's hiding shit from me. I can see it written all over his face. When people lie, they are far too obvious. Even him, a trained fucking assassin. He's no match for me.

"He's not anywhere near here," he spews as he tries to show off his false bravado that does nothing but annoy me.

Rolling my eyes, I chuckle. "Oh, I know he isn't. But you know where he is. So perhaps you should come clean."

"I'm here on another job. It has nothing to do—"

I push the knife in further, causing it to slice through flesh. Blood spurts from the wound, and the sound of an agonised scream echoes in my ears.

"See, now look what you made me do," I tell him as I smile.

Perhaps I'm a psychopath—I seem to be enjoying this just a little too much. It's been far too long since I let myself go. Over the weeks Brielle's been here, she's softened me. I need to find myself again.

Here he is... the crazy fucking psycho who likes to cut people up. I pull the knife from the dick of my captive, and I press it to his lips.

"If you open wide like a good boy, maybe I'll let you live."

This part of my job is always fun, watching

arseholes squirm as they try to act strong, but I can see they're not. I like it when they attempt to fight back. It's as if they want me to hurt them. And I'll gladly accept the challenge.

"Fuck you, Venier," he spits as his expression flashes rage.

It's exactly what I want. I'd a feeling he wouldn't spill anything, so I thrust the blade into his mouth and fuck his throat with it. Watching the metal slide over his tongue before it opens up the throat and then the neck.

I'm caked in crimson by the time I'm done, and I haven't been hard like this since the night I fucked Brielle in the shower.

I drop the knife on the metal tray and click my fingers. The men who accompanied me into the dungeon can clean this mess up. I have something better to be doing. I should have gone straight upstairs earlier, but I wanted to see if this piece of shit had anything useful for me. He didn't.

As I make my way back up through the house and take the stairs two at a time, I wonder what I'll find when I walk into Brielle's bedroom. She may think it belongs to her, but each room in this house has a history.

Hers…well, let's just say she isn't the first girl to get fucked in there, but she's the only one who won't be leaving in the morning.

She glances up at me when I walk in. I'm covered in blood, but I don't intend to explain. I don't give a shit what she thinks of me right now. I need to escape into the shadows and forget the world outside exists.

Without saying a word, I unbutton my shirt and allow it to fall to the floor. The clink of my belt echoes in the room as I lower my trousers and step out of them. Socks go next, but I leave my underwear on.

I'm not ready to be completely bared to her. Not again, anyway.

Her leg is still covered in a dressing from where she was shot. She's struggling to move easily, but as she lies back on the bed with Kai beside her, I enjoy the view of her body.

"She's going to be the ruin of us," Valen says softly from behind me, his lips whispering along my jaw. His warmth washes over me as I watch her with Kai.

We all know Brielle is a seductress. She walked into our lives and turned them upside down. I didn't expect to *want* to fall in love with her, but I find I can't stop myself craving every part of her. Every moment of every fucking day, it's exhausting.

"It scares you. Doesn't it?" Val whispers.

He knows me too well. I don't have to answer. My hardened cock throbs at the sight of Brielle's shimmering lips wrapped round Kai's erection. So many times, over the years, we've enjoyed sharing girls in this bedroom, but none of them were like Brielle. She's not a one-night stand. She's ours, and she's here to stay.

Valen's hand grips my dick through my boxers, and I stifle the groan of pleasure as he squeezes me then slowly strokes me over the material. Tonight, pleasures of the flesh can be explored and enjoyed, but come tomorrow morning, Brielle will be sent off to finalise the details of the wedding, our wedding.

There are details she needs to confirm, her dress needs to be finished, and I'm not even sure what the fuck else there is. But for tonight, we'll get lost in each other.

Desire is a dangerous game. It steals you from your everyday life, leading you into temptation you never thought you'd fall prey to. And yet, here I am, the cold-hearted bastard, with my best friends and the girl I want nothing more than to fuck and kill. Perhaps, even at the same time.

"She still needs to tell us more," I say as Valen teases precum from my dick. I'm leaking, throbbing, but I won't give in, not yet. The more I stay on edge, the better the orgasm will be.

"Are you joining us?" Kai calls, stealing both mine and Valen's attention.

"I will," I say as I smile at both men.

I was learning to trust her before those fucking goons walked into my home and tried to take her.

Even though we killed them, I know more will come. But it's because of her father that all this shit has gone down, which means Brielle must know something. She can't play the innocent card forever.

"Jude," Kai's voice drags me away from the thoughts racing through my mind.

I'm a fucking mess, thanks to her. Anger takes over, and I take a few steps towards the bed.

"Don't worry about me." My words have turned to ice.

I can tell both men know something is up, but Brielle is lost to the pleasure Valen is currently sending through her body as he teases the slick folds of her cunt with his fingers.

Her legs are spread open before me while Valen gently licks and devours her. Even in my anger, I can appreciate the beauty in front of me. The scene that's filled with desire and lust makes my cock ache.

Kai moves towards her once more, and she takes his shaft between her lips. The soft sucking sound makes the precum leak into my boxers.

They're enjoying the moment, and I can't stop my hand from slowly stroking my cock from base to tip. Moving behind Valen, I grip his arse, and squeeze both cheeks until I hear him moan against Brielle. There is nothing more I enjoy than the sounds of pleasure.

Brielle's already nearing orgasm as her body

bows off the bed, and I grab the lube and a condom from the bedside table and tease Valen with the cool liquid. Sheathing my cock, I grip the shaft, needing to be inside Val. The moment I feel he's ready, I poise my cock at the tight ring of muscle and inch into him. The sensations are incredible as pleasure races through my veins. His moan is louder now as I lift his hips.

Brielle has Kai's thick cock in her mouth, her lips stretched around it as she hums with delight while Valen's fingers fuck her. She slowly opens her eyes and looks at me before releasing Kai's cock from her mouth. She reaches for Valen's head, but he doesn't stop. He continues to devour her cunt until her body shudders from an orgasm that has her eyes rolling back.

I can't stop myself from nearing the edge as I slip from Valen. Keeping myself hard is easy as I watch the men swap places. Brielle is coming down from her high when she notices Valen's cock leaking and ready. He lifts her from the bed and shifts their bodies so he's under the pretty princess and she's facing him. He holds her against him, and Kai and I watch as his thick erection slips into her cunt.

It's a beautiful sight. Kai takes his position at her arse, and he toys with her until she's whimpering. His cock slowly enters her while I move to her mouth. She's going to take us all. Filled, claimed, and fucking owned.

"Fuck," I bite out as I thrust deeply into her mouth, and when I feel that gag reflex at the back of her throat, I smile.

Looking down at Brielle, I enjoy seeing those pretty eyes water with tears as she tries to take what I'm giving to her. I know she won't fight me as I reach for her neck and squeeze. It's a slight movement, not too tight, but it's enough to have my cock throbbing even harder as I feel her struggle to breathe.

When I pull my cock from her mouth, she coughs, pulling in much needed air. I smile as I lean forward, my mouth against her cheek.

"You're a pretty little thing when you can't breathe," I whisper, taunting her. "I think we all three need to take you. Helpless little spy."

"You're an arsehole, Judah," Brielle bites out, anger dripping from every word. But it only makes me smile wider.

Val and Kai continue to thrust inside her as I take her one hand, and bring it to my cock. "Most girls would kill to be with us." I tell her.

It's no word of a lie. So many students have wanted to come home with us. Over the years, we've chosen a few to join us in the bedroom. We've never revealed our proclivities though. We've always focused solely on pleasuring them, not each other.

I've never hurt a woman in my life, even when they've fucked up, and I won't break my moral code for Brielle, but she will come to know the darker side of me, especially once we're married.

Valen and Kai continue to fuck her earnestly, and I pull away, allowing her to enjoy the way they're using her. I lean in to kiss Valen, before I completely leave the bed, and settle in the armchair in the corner of the room.

I sit back, legs spread out in front of me as I stroke myself. Her eyes find mine, and I smirk when she looks at me as if she wants me to be right there with them. But I'm content here, hiding in the shadows, finding my release as they lose themselves in their own pleasures.

The room is filled with a symphony of sex. Moans and whimpers, grunts and groans. And it doesn't take long for all of us to find our release.

I push to my feet and walk out of the room. I've had enough for the night. Tomorrow, more secrets will be uncovered. All I can do is pray we're ready for them.

KILLING A PRINCE

BRIELLE

When I first arrived in Black Hollow, I didn't think my life would take the turn is has. And while the wedding is only a few days away, I can't stop thinking about the future. I've been ignoring all those worries for the past few months. But there's no more hiding now.

I can't turn away from the truth—I'm here under the pretext of marriage, but I received a message from my father yesterday, and I can't ignore him. He's my blood. But I've also fallen in love with the three men who've protected me since I walked onto this island.

"Are you ready?" The voice from behind me has me turning to find Valen.

It's been a welcome distraction having him around. Since the day I met him, Val has been a force of calm. He's not like the other two, he's got a sensitive side, but he only shows it to me. At first, I thought it was an act, but having seen him around others, around the students in his class, I realise I'm the only one he never hides it away from.

He's watched me blossom over the past three months, and now that we're here, with me standing in a white gown having the dressmaker pin and prod at the material, there's something in Valen's eyes.

"I don't know if I'll ever be ready," I tell him. "I thought this would be easier as time passed, but..." I allow my words to drift into nothing as I'm finally done and able to get out of the dress.

Valen helps me down from the podium, and I quickly slip on a dressing gown. His hands grip my upper arms, and he holds me steady. When I glance up, I notice an emotion in his expression I didn't see when he walked in.

"If there is anything bothering you," Valen says as he looks at me. "You'll tell me. Won't you?"

It's now or never. I could admit the truth, I could tell him everything that's been eating away at me since yesterday, but I know it won't do any good. It won't change my father's plans.

All my life I thought Papa saw me as more than a pawn in a game. I grew up with him training me in ways that now make sense. Back then, I was just proud to have his attention. My mother left when I was very young, so it was only us, and I wanted my papa to love me.

And he did.

But now he expects me to obey him and go against everything I've come to love, I'm struggling. And Valen can see it written all over my face. Of the three men in my life, Valen is the one I'm closest to. Well, he's the one who's able to read me the best.

If I was anywhere near Judah, I know he'd sense something was amiss, but he wouldn't worry about me. I think he sees me as an equal now. The queen to his king. Where as Valen still sees the girl.

"Nothing is wrong," I finally lie.

The words taste like poison on my lips, but there's nothing more I can say. Either way, someone is going to die tomorrow, and I just need to make sure I'm there to stop the war that's about to shatter my world.

"I've come to know you rather well, princess," Valen says, his voice taking on a tone I've only ever heard him use with his students. Almost as cold as Judah's. "Lying isn't your strong suit."

I want to tell him everything, but I don't want to betray my father. If I do, I'll have to live with the guilt, but then I look at Valen. I meet his gaze, and I see the love and affection he holds for me. The Princes didn't have to accept me, to trust me, or to allow me into their private world. I would never tell anyone their secret, because it's not my story to tell. However, right now it feels as if I'm being ripped in two.

"There have been times in my life when I thought I had escaped this world," I tell him. "I knew my father walked away from the protection of the mafia. But he never once told me the *real* reasons, and I suppose in many respects, I was too naive to question him."

"Come," Valen says suddenly, and he leads me from the library, where I was getting my fitting done, and into Judah's office.

The room is empty of the usual guards and Capos, but there, behind his desk, is the man who will soon be my husband.

"What's going on?" he asks, leaning back in his large, white leather office chair. He's in a crisp blue shirt, the top three buttons undone, and the long sleeves rolled up to his elbows. His tanned skin's a bit darker now that summer is here, and the corded veins are obvious as he fists his hands at our interference.

He doesn't always say what he's thinking, but he's getting better at it. However, he doesn't need to say a word for it to be clear we've interrupted him.

"Show her," Valen says as we stop at the opposite side of Judah's desk. "She needs to see the truth, and if you don't show her, I will."

I'm not sure what he's talking about, but Judah doesn't look at all pleased.

Judah's gaze lands on mine, and for a long moment, I'm sure he's going to refuse. But then he sighs.

"Sit," he orders.

As always, his detached demeanour is evident. There have been moments, over the past few weeks, where I've seen Judah let his guard down. It's been refreshing, different, but for the most part, I've come to love his icy presence—the chill he exudes most of the time. However, when he's passionate, he's like a fire that rages through a forest, unyielding and dangerous.

A contrast if ever I saw one.

I settle in the chair and wait. There are so many things racing through my mind. With a quick glance at the balcony, I try to calm my erratic heartbeat, but it's useless. Perhaps I should tell him, confess. He'll be angry, but at least I won't be hiding things from him anymore.

Maybe I'll wait until he tells me whatever it is he needs to, and then I can come clean. I'm not sure what to expect when he looks at me, because there's no hint in his expression as to what this could be about.

My stomach flutters with the wings of a hummingbird. Judah pulls out a thick folder, heavy with what I assume are documents, but I'm uncertain what they'll reveal. More than likely, they contain evidence. Things I don't know but need to know. Secrets.

"You need to read through the contents of this file. Take your time going through the documents," he says. "If you have any questions, ask. There's a lot of information in there. Some things you may not *want* to know, but since you're about to walk down the aisle with me, it's best you learn it all."

"What is it?" I ask as I flick open the cover, and gasp when I see my father's name and photo on the first page. "This is… I mean…"

When I scan the page, my heart comes to a stop for a split second. I pray my hands don't shake—I force myself to stay calm. Judah is trained in reading people, and he'll see right through me if I convey any inclination as to the real reason I'm here.

"It's all the information we have on your father. It dates all the way back to when he was a child. There are some very interesting facts in there, Brielle." Judah pushes to his feet and rounds the desk. He's so close, I can feel his anger radiating from him. But I don't look up at the man I'm meant to marry, because I'm too afraid. I'm not frightened that he'll hurt me, but that he'll see the worry in my eyes. "It's also all the information we have on you, little spy."

They know. He knows. I can't face him, so I focus

on the pages in front of me. If I meet his inquisitive stare that's slowly burning a hole through me, he'll realise that everything I've told him is a lie. *But he already knows, Brielle.*

I flick to the last few pages where all my details are filed. Everything from when I was born, right up until I was brought to Black Hollow. And when I find the photos of Marco and me, I know my time is up. I'm going to die today.

"This is my past," I say, trying to keep my voice as even as I possibly can. It's not easy with my heart slamming against my rib cage. "There have been things I've had to do—the same as all of you. It's not been by choice. It was forced upon me, just like this marriage was. If you can't believe that, then I'm not sure what to tell you. There's nothing more I can say. You know—"

"I know you're a liar," Judah tells me as he leans in close, his warm breath fanning against my ear. Those piercing, hazel eyes drill through me with every second that passes. "You walked into this house, acted the sweet and innocent little princess, but what I've discovered is you're nothing more than a trained fucking soldier for your father."

I push to my feet in a show of fake confidence because all I feel now is fear. I walked into the lion's den knowingly. Granted, the full plan was only revealed to me last night, so I didn't know my father was watching, listening. After I killed Marco, I thought I was safe. But I should have known that when you're amongst hunters, you're never truly safe.

I throw the folder back onto the desk and take a step towards Judah.

"If you believe that, why not kill me?" I challenge him.

This time, I do look at him. I meet those pretty eyes that have captured me since I first saw them. Now they hold an emotion I've never seen in them before—betrayal. I've hurt Judah. I didn't think that would ever be possible.

"I don't kill women," he throws back at me before gripping my arm and dragging me to the balcony doors.

He shoves them open and pulls me out onto the landing. It's cold out, and I can't stop the shiver that wracks through me.

He shouldn't be out here. I try to pull away, try to turn around because panic slowly settles in my gut. The email I received today on my phone was clear. I didn't mean for this to happen, I didn't think he would bring me out here, but Judah is a loose cannon at times.

"Take me inside," I bite out in frustration, but he doesn't listen.

He spins me around, my back to his front. He

leans against me, our bodies flush, the heat of him making me want to move in closer. But I can't, because I'm sure he knows about the plan.

"You see, little spy," he whispers along the shell of my ear. "When your father thought he could outsmart a future Boss, no, not one Boss but three, he was sorely mistaken."

"I-I-I don't know what you mean," I whisper as Judah's teeth capture my earlobe, and he bites down until waves of electric currents shoot through me, from the top of my head right down to my toes. There's something pleasurable about the danger he's emanating.

His hand trails up my side, but I don't move. There's no reason to fight him anymore, because it's clear he does know. It's why he brought me out here. I thought killing a Prince would be easier than this.

Papa told me it would be simple. All I had to do was infiltrate the Venier mansion and discover their secrets. And I was close to succeeding. So fucking close.

"I knew you weren't an innocent, little whore," Judah whispers. "But you wanted me to find out. Didn't you?"

His hand snakes up to my throat, and I know, somewhere in the shadows, whoever Papa hired can see us. Maybe my father is out there too. Knowing he could be watching what Judah's doing to me sends shame racing through me.

"Judah, stop," I tell him, but I know he won't listen. He's angry. He feels betrayed, but he doesn't know the whole story.

His other hand pushes between my thighs, and I almost collapse from the friction. Desire and fear dance a tango inside me, swirling as his fingers wrap around my throat while his others tease my core over the material of my leggings until I'm shaking.

"Do you want me to stop?" he questions as he circles my clit with his thumb.

It doesn't matter about the threat of danger. His touch sends shockwaves through me.

"N-No," I mumble as my lashes flutter.

"I think your precious papa is out there, watching you lose yourself to a Prince. He's looking at his daughter, and he's probably repulsed by you right now."

"He loves me," I bite back, knowing I've made mistakes in the past, but Papa has always been there for me.

Judah dips his hand into my leggings and beneath my underwear. He chuckles when he finds me wet, and his expert touch pushes me closer to the edge. He knows what he's doing, and he's enjoying it because I can feel his hardness against my back.

"You should feel ashamed that you're loving this so much."

His words are meant to hurt, to taunt, to get me raging against him, and I want to. I want to pummel him right now, but the deeper he sinks his fingers inside me, the tighter his hold on my neck gets.

"Fuck you, Judah," I bite out, knowing that no matter how much I try to fight it, I have feelings for Judah, and for Val and Kai.

I see them in a different light now, not as the Lawless Princes they claim to be, but I see them as strong, loyal, handsome men. I see them as friends and lovers.

Judah's fingers tease my clit before he pinches the hardened nub, sending me over the edge. Feeling dizzy from my orgasm, I cry out as my head falls back against his shoulder. Pleasure races through me as I tremble. And as I'm lost in the bliss, a deafening gunshot rings out. It startles me back to the present, and I know without intending to betray Judah that I've done so.

And, if he survives, he'll never forgive me.

RUTHLESS KINGS - SNEAK PEEK

JUDAH

We're going to be the Ruthless Kings soon. It's a name that will be bestowed on us when we step up to the thrones of our families. I thought we would have a Queen beside us, but she lied.

She hid things from me I can never forgive. And now, I will walk on this journey with only Valen and Kai.

I don't love her.

I never felt anything for her.

That's the same mantra I tell myself every single fucking day.

But I know it's all a lie.

Preorder Ruthless Kings today!

SNEAK PEEK - VENGEANCE OF THE FALLEN

If you're waiting on Ruthless Kings, why not dive into my other why choose romance, Vengeance of the Fallen?

Keep reading for a snippet, or order it now only on Amazon and find it in Kindle Unlimited!

PREFACE

CROW

Nobody starts their life out as a killer.

No child wakes up one morning and announces he's going to become a hitman.

But that's where life has brought me. It's in the eyes of my brothers in arms I find my humanity. If you can even call it that.

We've all three witnessed atrocities, and when we watched these violent acts unfolding, it wasn't on a television screen, it was real life. Perhaps it's why my mind broke. I'm certain it's why Falcon and Hawk, my brothers by all standards that matter, hunger for the same revenge that I need.

We may not be blood, but we're family all the same.

They are the only people I trust with my life. Because they know how precious it is. Being alive, it's a gift, one that can be taken at any moment. It has brought us to the work we do. We know how to steal those last moments of someone's light and snuff it out as if they'd never existed.

Most people who know us, fear us—and they should.

We can empty your bank account, find every dark, sordid secret you've ever had hidden away, and we'll do it so we can get our payday. When your life is gone, there is no getting it back. Most times, we don't have to kill those we're hired to because once we're done they want to die anyway.

It makes our lives much easier.

Wealthy people hire us to do their dirty work, and I don't mind. I like to get my hands filthy. There's honesty in what I do. With a swipe of my blade, with the pull of a trigger, I can take out anyone who stands in my way.

There is only one person who I haven't killed yet, and it's not for the lack of trying. He's locked up tight in prison. I know he'll get out; he has connections. One day, and I know the day will come, I'll look him in the eye and watch the life drain from his face.

I want to bathe in his blood. It will be sweet vengeance.

In the darkness of the living room, I move to the balcony with a cigarette pressed between my lips. Outside, I flick the lighter and take a long, deep inhale. It's as if I can *see* the smoke curling around my nerves, collecting in my lungs, and when I breathe it out, it billows like a cloud.

The apartment is draped in darkness, and I blend into my surroundings, dressed all in black as I stand guard. My watchful gaze is trained on the building across from me. I can see her moving around her flat. She's oblivious to me. But she'll soon learn danger lurks in the shadows.

Each night I come to the apartment we bought in the city only to watch her. This is our ticket to the one thing we've been wanting for years. At first, Falcon was concerned about my plan, but when I told him she's the spawn of the most evil man we'd ever come across, he agreed.

I kept her a secret for months before I told my brothers. Something I have never done before. They know everything there is to know about me. I can't explain it, but there is something about her I want to keep to myself. A piece of her which calls to me.

A pretty little blonde with angel eyes and pouty lips. Her body is sinful. Perhaps it's the reason why I didn't tell my brothers. Because I know the moment Falcon sees her, he'll want to enjoy every curve.

My blood heats as she moves to the second bedroom of her apartment where she'll log into her computer, touch herself, and come. Her orgasm will be real, and she'll slowly come down from her high.

But deep down the guilt will eat away at her like it does every time she does it. I watch the way she rushes from the room afterward. It happens at least twice a week. She'll run to the main bedroom, cover herself in a robe, and curl up on a chair by the window as tears streak her cheeks.

Our Goldilocks is broken in ways I didn't fathom. I had no idea what was going on the first few times it happened. It doesn't stop my need to make her pay. Even if she begs for her life, she owes me one back. And I intend on taking.

I know who she really is.

I know what she did.

Meet The Fallen today!

ALSO BY DANI RENÉ

Click here for a full list of Dani René's incredible titles

ABOUT THE AUTHOR

Dani is a *USA Today* Bestselling Author of seductive and deviant romance.

Her books range from the dark to emotional, but every hero is alpha, and each heroine is strong-willed, bringing the men down to their knees.

She now lives in the UK, after moving from Cape Town, exploring cemeteries and old buildings while plotting her next book.

When she's not writing, she can be found binge-watching the latest TV series, or working on graphic design. She has a healthy addiction to reading, tattoos, coffee, and ice cream.

www.danirene.com
info@danirene.com
Spotify